I0713463

VOYAGE OF THE DREADNAUGHT

Four Stella Madison Capers

Including:
SEA TRIALS
THE PUSHOVER PLOT
LOST IN THE WILDERNESS
THE LAST RESORT

Lilly Maytree

LIGHTSMITH PUBLISHERS
Thorne Bay, Alaska

LIGHTSMITH PUBLISHERS
P.O. Box 19293
Thorne Bay, AK 99919
www.LightsmithPublishers.com

Ordering Information:
Quantity sales. Special discounts are available on quantity purchases by corporations, associations, and others. For details, contact the "Special Sales Department" at the address above.

Voyage of the Dreadnaught/ Lilly Maytree. 1st Edition

ISBN: 978-1-944798-06-2

Contents

What Happened First...

Stella Madison did not set out to live a life of capers. Nobody does. But sooner, or later everyone faces one of some kind, or another. The fact is, we all run into troubles occasionally, no matter who we are. For Stella, it happened when she was unexpectedly dumped out of a quiet retirement and forced to go back to work just to make ends meet. But having grown rusty on her people skills and coming from a different generation altogether, it was practically murder. Anyway, that's what she was accused of when things were at their worst. However, a true hero came to her rescue and that changed everything. It was also during that time she met Colonel Oliver P. Henry (retired), who always believes the best of her. (*Home Before Dark*)

After that, things changed tremendously for the better. Stella took an apartment next to the colonel, which was situated in an old Hollywood mansion that had seen better days, and had been remodeled to ccommodate multiple dwellings. Such charm, and she absolutely loved it. Best of all, it was affordable. The others who lived there were rather odd (in a likable sort of way) and she was supremely happy. For a little over two months.

At which point, there was another run of trouble when owners of the place declared intentions to sell, announced they would be coming by to take inventory, and no one had ever informed them about the remodel. Worse yet, it was discovered there was a thief in the house who had been selling off the more expensive "Golden Era" artifacts for some years. During this time, Stella realizes she has changed a lot since her last catastrophe and makes a decision she would never even have considered before. (*A Thief in the House*)

That's how it happened that Stella Madison became committed (in more ways than one) to a rag-tag group of misfits who decided to pool their resources and make a run for an abandoned lodge in Alaska. Where it is rumored seniors do not have to pay taxes and it is possible to survive completely off the land, even if they have no income, at all. At the very least, they would fare better than each trying to fend for themselves. Times being what they were.

The only real expense was getting there. However, one of the group is acquainted with an old captain-turned-inventor who lives out in the bay on a monstrosity of a sailboat called the *Dreadnaught*. And while it hasn't been out of the harbor in years, it does fall within their budget to charter it. That is, if they skip the extra expense of a crew and all sign on as hands. Even though Stella has never been out on a boat in her life...

"The longer I live, the more convincing proofs I see of this truth – that God governs in the affairs of men."

Benjamin Franklin

Sea Trials

A Stella Madison Caper

Stella Madison flinched when a cold splash of spray hit her face and she tightened her hold on the bouncing rail. The motorboat was loaded to full capacity, with Colonel Oliver P. Henry's large bulk ensconced precisely in the middle for better balance. She and her friend Millie (who had insisted on wearing a bright orange life preserver) were at the very front, practically hanging over the bow. Gerald and Lou were in the last seat behind the Colonel, while the Captain stood up in the stern with a casual grip on the tiller and the outboard turned up to full throttle. The Senator was riding like a king in a backpack-type apparatus attached to his mother.

"E-gads!" Gerald complained as they bounced off another ripple of chop and sped through the darkness. "I say – is it necessary to go all out?"

"It is if we want to get out of this bay before ten o'clock," answered Captain Stewart, whose gray hair was standing up all over like wild man in the wind.

It was six thirty-seven in the morning. On a Sunday.

Just as Stella began to wonder what in the world she had let herself in for, Stuart cut the motor to half-power and they spent the next ten minutes weaving in and out around the dark shapes and shadows of other boats anchored across the bay. The sky was still black as night. While her hurried breakfast of donuts and coffee was beginning to churn with a mind of its own, a great ominous wall gradually emerged out of the darkness. The Captain turned the little craft smartly, and cut the motor. He tossed a line over a cleat as they drifted up against a floating wooden platform, and then jumped out to run forward and secure the bow.

"Here we are, mates!" he crowed. "Go easy – one at a time, now – it's too early to have to fish anybody out of the water!"

Stella climbed out and stepped gingerly onto the rocking platform with a distinct sense of vertigo and nothing to hang on to. Just as she began to sink to her knees to keep from falling, she felt Captain Stuart's strong grasp under her arm and he propelled her forward to a dangling metal stairway. It stretched diagonally up against the wall – who cared where it went – as long as it took her away from here. She clutched the cold wet rail and began to climb. If she had tried to wait for the Colonel, she fully believed she would have vomited.

There was a light on at the top and she recognized Millie's carpenter friend, Mason, as he reached out to help her step up and over onto the deck. At least she thought it was a deck. What it looked like was some narrow alleyway in the industrial section of the city, along with a row of metal doorways with round windows that disappeared somewhere outside the feeble circle of light over the stairs.

"Top o'the morning, Stella!" Mason said with a contrived accent and obvious excitement for the occasion.

"Oh, Mase! You better help Lou – I don't know how she's going to cart that baby of hers all the way up here!"

"She's in better shape than any of us, old girl. But don't worry, she's used to it. We come out here every Fourth of July to watch the fireworks. Last time she was pregnant, so this time she'll think it's a breeze. Here comes Mil."

Millie handed over a large picnic basket, packed to the brim while she maneuvered out of her orange life preserver. "Hi, Mase – been up all night?"

"Well, it happens I have, and I could sure use a--"

"Come on, Stella!" Her friend beamed as if the excitement were infectious. "I'll show you the galley – you'll just love it!"

The *Dreadnaught* was a monstrous old schooner nearly eighty feet long that looked as if it had been around since the early days of sail. Over the years it had by turns been used to carry cargo, transport passengers, and had even done a stint in the fishing trade. Though it still sported an entire set of working canvas, it had once run on steam, but—somewhere down the line—been converted over to diesel. To Stella, it looked like some ancient but perpetual work in progress. But Millie was right about the galley.

It boasted a magnificent iron cook-stove that was plumbed for propane (but could also burn wood), a huge wooden table carved out of genuine Philippine mahogany set between large comfortable settees that (even though faded and grease-stained) had once been covered in an expensive burgundy plush. Above it hung a fancy brass lantern that swung gently back and forth to the barely perceptible rocking of the sea beneath them. Plenty of counter space. Two deep stainless steel sinks that were every cook's dream…and the cupboards! Stella was sure such storage could never be found in a kitchen on land.

As if that weren't enough, there was a walk-in pantry the size of a small room just for laying in food supplies. According to Millie. At the moment, Stuart was using it as a paint locker.

"I'm going to take this cabin, here," Millie dragged her – still gawking – through a shuttered wooden door with an adorable brass knob that was just to the left of the stove. "Cook's quarters. What do you think?"

It was at that moment Stella was bitten with the same infectious excitement she had seen in all the others. Why it was another trip back in time! Like *Casablanca* and the *Orient Express* all rolled into one. An exotic little stateroom with mahogany woodwork all around; a bed off in one corner that sported (though faded and dusty) a palm-print spread; and a round brass porthole that opened right up over the sea. Stella could tell because she caught a waft of the moist salt air coming through.

"There's even enough room to set up my favorite rocker." Millie pointed to an area near the porthole, as she refastened her thick auburn hair back up into the clip the long strands had sprung loose from. "I can't wait to get all my things in."

"I had no idea!"

"Let's go look at the Captain's quarters." With cheeks still flushed from the early morning boat ride, Millie propelled her reluctantly back through the galley and down some long interior companionway. "It's where you and the Colonel get to stay."

"What?" Stella felt her own color rising at the thought, and wondered how long it would take to get used to the fact she was Mrs. Oliver P. Henry, now. Married to a colonel (retired) who had spent his career as a military historian. Obviously more than twenty-four hours.

"Stella, it's the perfect place for newlyweds. Just wait till you see this!"

"If that's the case, why don't you and Mason get the honor?"

"Are you kidding? I love him but we need our space. We'd be at each other's throats if we actually had to live together. Know what I mean?"

"Not really. But what about Stuart, then? He's the Captain, isn't he? Why doesn't he take the best apartment?"

"Stewart's something of an inventor. Always tinkering and making modifications on his engine. He wouldn't be happy anywhere but down in the engine room in the Chief Engineer's cabin. Been down there for years, and all this just stays empty. He's even got television down there!"

The companionway grew darker the farther they moved away from the light in the galley, but Millie seemed to know where she was going and kept plowing ahead with Stella still in tow. At the end of the narrow hallway, a few moments were devoted to pushing open a thick wooden door that obviously hadn't been moved for ages.

"It'll take some cleaning up, of course," Millie switched on a light attached to the nearest wall that sported a tattered red shade with tassels, right out of the era of speak-easies and bootleg liquor. "But did you ever see such extravagance?"

Extravagance wasn't the word for it.

The paneling was a rich mahogany, inlaid with

various mermaids and sea creatures over each doorway and window. Half the back wall was a slanted bank of French windows, complete with tufted window seat beneath. Stella could just make out the outline of the sea from the faint glow of dawn that was beginning to spread over the sky. Beneath that was a gray plaid sofa with carved wooden curlicues arching over the back and arms, to end in feet that were bolted to the floor. Part of the wooden floor was covered over by a gaudy red and black Oriental rug that also seemed to be tacked down.

There was a huge desk off in one corner with a leather swivel chair behind – Oliver would like that, no doubt – the perfect place to sit and work by the hour without missing what the weather was behaving like outside, or hear what was happening up on the decks above. And for Stella, there were bookshelves everywhere. Only a few scattered and dusty volumes tipped over to occupy them now, but she could already foresee her own collection displayed in a comforting array all around, just waiting to be perused on dull evenings. The last thing she had expected on this venture was luxury. Things were definitely looking up.

Her eye traveled across to the wall opposite the desk, and there was the most –

"There you are!" Mason's voice boomed from the open doorway, where he stood with a half-finished chicken leg in hand. "Stuart wants everyone to--"

"Mason Jefferies!" Millie complained, "It's too early to be digging into the lunch!"

"But I'm half-starved, Mil. Been up working most of the night, and the only food ol' Stuart keeps around here are sardines and crackers, or boiled eggs. A man's got to have more than--"

"Oh, come on, then, and I'll fix you a ham sandwich."
She headed back down the hall toward the galley.

"Stuart wants us all up on deck in about ten minutes,
Stella," he said before turning to follow Millie. "So we
can get started."

"All right," Stella answered. "I'll be along in a
minute."

This because she needed another minute to finish
exploring her new home, and maybe pinch herself once,
or twice, to make certain this was all really happening.
There was something "other worldly" about the place –
no denying it – and the sudden feeling of "déjà vu" she
experienced the moment she was left alone, proved it.
How else could everything feel so familiar? Take that
darling little wood-burning stove, for instance.

She knew exactly how it worked already. One simply
lifted the small iron handle from its perch near the black
pipe that went up through the ceiling, and used the hook
end to lift one of the round burner covers that lead to the
firebox below. Then one could regulate the amount of
flame or coals necessary to –

She dropped the iron ring and jumped back as if it had
burned her. And there it was, another one of those
stabbing memories that came and went so fast one
couldn't quite make it out. Along with the full-blown
vision of a woman. But she had never seen such a woman!
A beautiful young woman lifting one of the lids to that
stove, with her dark hair all done up like one of the old-
fashioned Gibson Girls. But she was wearing a man's
clothes and there was a cigarette dangling from one
corner of her mouth…

Impossible! It was all in her mind – it had to be – for there was no one else standing at this cold little stove that obviously hadn't been lit for years. "Oh, dear--" she murmured to herself, as she slowly backed away from it. "Surely not this, again – not now!" No doubt it was the stress and strain of having to move, again, so soon. That's what it had to be.

"Are you all right, my dear?" How long had the Colonel been standing behind her? "Not feeling seasick, are you?"

"Not any more," Stella replied with a quick smile. "What do you think, Oliver? These are the Captain's quarters and everyone decided you and I should move in here."

"Magnificent desk!" He went over to try out the leather-upholstered chair and open and close a few of the drawers. "Comfortable, too. I have a feeling I could do my best work here, Stel."

"Oh, I know you can!" How distinguished he looked sitting there with that head of gray curls, his deep tan, and such a delightfully comfortable gaze. A lot more like a captain than that grizzly old Stuart. "And it will be even better by the time I get it all fixed up for us. Wait and see. I have to admit I was a little skeptical when we first came aboard but I'm thoroughly won over, now. I caught the fever from Millie."

"Sea fever?"

"Well, traveling fever, anyway." She took her purse off her shoulder and pulled a red bandana from one of its pockets to tie around her hair. She had a feeling the short white fluff that normally framed her face and tucked under neatly at the back, must be standing on end about as much as Captain Suart's was on that wild ride across the bay. "Don't know what kind of crew member I'll end up making but I'll certainly give it my best shot."

"As you do everything, my dear. It's one of the things I like best about you." He got to his feet. "Now, I suppose we should get back out on deck before Stuart starts bellowing orders."

Stella had not been put to so much physical exertion since the early days of her single life, when she was a substitute for high school P.E. Up with the sails, down with the sails, heave ho, and prepare to come about! Over and over again until she thought she was beginning to see double. What's more, these were enormous sails that took at least two of them to fully raise. Nobody was in shape.

Except maybe Stuart, who kept popping up unexpectedly in one place or another to bawl, "Harder! Put some back into it! We're trying to sail here – not set up tents! Blast it – Gerald – you're out of sink with everybody, again. Let's do it over!" And in the meanwhile, steering the boat, tending or shutting down the engine, and generally running circles around everybody.

When they broke for lunch at noon, everyone was so exhausted there were serious doubts about the whole endeavor. Only the baby seemed to be in his element, swinging contentedly between the starboard rail and a cabin corner, harnessed into some bouncing contraption called a "Johnny Jumper" that Mason had jury-rigged for him to play in. Millie's efforts at serving lunch amounted to little more than flopping open the top of the picnic basket and letting everyone fend for themselves. After that they were all granted a bit of "liberty" to regain their composure.

The *Dreadnaught* was anchored just far enough out in the channel to make the city and surrounding mountains look picture perfect nestled between a blue sky and slate green sea. Stella knew they were "at anchor" because they had dropped and hauled the thing back in again, at least four times during training maneuvers. She knew starboard was right and port was left, and forward and aft meant front and back respectively. Now all time seemed to be suspended in its tracks just to wait for them to pick things up again.

Everything felt incredibly peaceful.

What little wind there had been in the morning was almost completely gone and the sea was in a state of such flat calm inside the bay that she had to try very hard to feel even the slightest twinge of seasickness. After Lou settled the Senator down with an exhausted Gerald (who performed quite remarkably for someone living on disability) for a nap in one of the main deck cabins, she returned to where Stuart was tinkering with something mechanical back on the afterdeck.

"Can I fish for a while, Cap?" She set an icy can of root beer down on the deck beside him, and popped the top off an orange soda for herself.

"Didn't bring any bait this trip."

"How 'bout I use a chicken bone?"

"Suit yourself. You know where everything is."

Stella sipped at her cold tea and watched from the comfort of a faded blue deck chair pulled out into the sun. The Colonel was dozing in another deck chair beside her with his feet propped up on a nearby winch drum and his head leaned back against the smooth teak railing in front of the row of cabins. Millie had retired to her cook's quarters, and she had no idea where Mason had disappeared.

"I'm going to catch you a big yellow tail tuna for supper," Lou Edna announced.

"I'll wager five bucks you won't catch anything but mackerel, barracuda, or shark with that stuff," Stuart replied without looking up from his project. "Ain't any of which I like to eat."

"Orientals eat all those things," the young woman bantered.

"Yeah, and they eat bugs and rodents, too."

"Prejudiced, are you?"

"Not me. I was married to a Japanese gal once after the War. Doesn't mean I have to like eating junk food though."

"Junk food!" Lou Edna laughed and ignored the thin strap of her green tank top that slipped off her shoulder as she cast her line over the rail. "This generation junk food means a hamburger and fries."

"Now them I like."

Stella didn't quite know what to make of Lou Edna. The lies and taking advantage of Millie with rent and babysitting money had made her feel critical of the girl, at first. On the other hand, she was clearly attached to them all, as if Millie and Mason were surrogate parents and Gerald some favorite Uncle. The Colonel she seemed a bit wary of. Probably because he was indifferent to the ruses she used so freely on the others and made no effort to play along with her games. But for the most part she was polite with him.

Watching her easy banter with Stuart – Stella couldn't help wondering what the girl was really after. Because it was obvious this supple blonde-haired beauty that smelled all over like tanning oil today, was definitely after something. Stella had seen enough of her kind in the high schools she used to teach in to practically recognize them on sight.

Yes, Lou Edna was after something. The tears of last night had come and gone too quickly for such a hardened student of the rough life. Millie had also mentioned something about the girl having been raised in a long series of foster homes. But what really had Stella stumped was that it just didn't seem right how someone with the responsibility of a baby could so flippantly leave a decent paying job to trot off into the unknown where there might not be any job waiting at all. Did she think the "family" would simply take care of her and the Senator indefinitely? Stella could see how they all probably would, though, because that baby was about as cute as they came.

With a sudden squeal of delight that ended in a peal of musical laughter, Lou Edna began reeling in her line as fast as she could. It had been out there less than ten minutes. Just when Stella was thinking these waters must be teaming with fish, Lou tossed the empty pole down on the deck and proceeded to bounce up and down along the length of the rail as she waved at someone in the far off distance.

"Over here!" she cupped her hands to her mouth and yelled. "Woooo-hoo! Over here, Cole!"

Which brought the Colonel awake with a start, and the Captain to his feet to see who it was. Stella got up, too, arriving at the rail just in time to catch sight of an open speedboat that came smartly up alongside and cut the motor.

"Hey–" said a dark-haired young man with a beautiful smile who was sitting on the seat back instead of the cushion as he drove. "Looks like I found you."

"You sure did!" beamed Lou. "Got any ideas? This old man here's working my tail off. On a Sunday, too!"

"Want to drive out to one of the islands?"

"She's putting in for a position," Stuart answered for her, "and I haven't decided, yet."

"Oh, come on, Cap…" Lou Edna leaned against the older man and lowered her voice in a confidential whisper. "You know I've got everything down already, and I'm the strongest deckhand you've got so far. Right?"

"Well…"

"I need a little fun before I leave."

"What kind of fun?" Mason came up behind them and cast a glance over the rail. "Who the devil's that?"

"Cole Deforio." The young man gave a nod of his head then turned his brown eyes back to Lou. "You coming, or not?"

"Sure, but I have to wait until the Senator wakes up. Why don't you come aboard and meet everybody?"

"I'd be happy to watch him for you, Lou," Stella interjected quickly – the thought of taking a baby into that miniscule little boat! "If you'd like to go on, that is. Seems a long trip to be starting out so late in a small open boat like that." Why, she had heard it was nearly six miles across open ocean even to get to the nearest island. After the bumpy adventure she had personally experienced this morning just crossing the calm harbor, the entire idea was appalling.

"Oh, would you, Stel? That would be great! He hasn't been feeling the best lately, anyway. I think he's got a bug, or something."

"No doubt."

"OK, change of plans – I'm coming down." Lou Edna reached for the black windbreaker she had tossed onto the deck earlier and fairly skipped toward the bow. "Pick me up under the anchor chain," she called over the noise of the motor as her young man started the engine, again. "And don't you dare let me fall in!"

Naturally, everyone followed. They lined up along the rail to watch her crawl up and over with an agility only the young possessed. As Cole expertly maneuvered his little boat directly under the apex of the chain and the bow, Lou made contact first with her feet and then lowered herself onto his shoulders with a playful giggle. He let the engine idle in neutral while he eased her down in a slow seductive slide against the front of his body that ended in a sizzling kiss no self-respecting person would engage in while others were watching.

"Dear heaven!" Stella fumed as the outboard revved into gear and they sped away. "And in broad daylight, too!"

"Somebody ought to knock some sense into that girl," Mason growled irritably. "Little flirt – what'd you let her go for, Stuart? Should have made her stay and suffer along with the rest of us."

"Well, I would have," the Captain was still watching the small boat as it receded into the horizon. "Only she's right. She is the best deckhand I got going for me on this trip."

"Who is that kid anyway?" Mason squinted into the sun as if he might be able to tell if he kept looking hard enough. "I've never seen him before."

"Been hanging around the docks the last couple months," Stuart replied. "Does a bit of work with the fleet now and again. Came in on one of them cargo boats before that."

"I wouldn't be surprised if he was the devil's own cousin," Stella pronounced. "And to think she was going to take the baby along!"

"Rather strange he knew right where to find us." The Colonel twisted the top off a bottle of chilled tea and drank half of it down without stopping.

Stella couldn't help thinking how at home he looked in this environment, with his khaki shorts, and Hawaiian shirt hanging loose and unbuttoned to reveal a thatch of curly gray hair. He must have spent a great deal of time at the beach over the years.

"Strange or not," Stuart turned away from the rail and headed back toward his project, "did you see them muscles? I could use a good hand like that on this trip."

"Good Grief!" the Colonel muttered to himself. "Then we'd really have problems to contend with!"

"Two of them acting like that night and day, nobody would miss the movies," Stuart chuckled.

Mason suddenly stood up straighter and shielded his eyes as he tried to catch a last glimpse. "Just what I thought… circling right back to shore."

Packing up an apartment was nothing compared to packing up a mansion. Especially one that had been lived in for nearly twenty years. True, very few of the Villa's furnishings actually belonged to Millie, but Stella soon discovered that the latter years of financial troubles had turned her newfound friend into a packrat. Specifically in the food department.

"What in the world!" Stella retied her red bandana to fit more snuggly around her ears as she stood gazing into a wine cellar that was stacked almost to the ceiling with a veritable mountain of food.

"It's my famine chest," Millie explained as she dragged a stack of plastic storage bins up close to the nearest edge. "Left over from our prepper years. Sam was one of those survivalist types that thought World War III was going to break out any day. Either that, or the California coastline was going to drop off into the ocean during the hundred year biggie."

"The hundred year biggie?"

"You know – the big one. The next earthquake that measures over eight points to hit smack along the San Andreas fault. We even have a stash of guns and ammunition in case we ever have to defend ourselves when total chaos breaks loose in the cities."

"Goodness–it must have cost a fortune!"

"Not exactly. Sam was a real wheeler-dealer. Before he left me, we always had plenty of money. Here. You can take half of these bins and start on that end while I get busy on this one."

Stella retreated to her specified area and began to pack can after can of condensed soup and beef stew into the containers. "This hardly looks like your cupboards, Mil… you being such a stickler for cooking fresh from scratch and all."

"In case of a real emergency, there's not always a working kitchen at hand," Millie explained. "Look at all the people who were stranded in their own front yards after that last big one. Water lines broke. All the power went out. Streets and highways were busted or buckled in so many places you couldn't even drive out."

She stopped for a moment as if remembering and then shook off the memory to get back to work. "Nope. The houses were too dangerous to stay in, so–what with the aftershocks going off for days afterward--most people were stuck camping out in their own front yards with whatever they had on hand in their cupboards. Which this day and age isn't much considering how almost everybody works and eats out most of the time."

"It's true -- hardly anyone cooks at home anymore," Stella agreed. "I had a neighbor back at my old apartment complex who was always dieting, so she didn't want any food around her place at all. Just went to the grocery store every day or so, and ate out every night."

"A lot of people do. Anyway, that's why most of this stuff you can just open up and eat cold right out of the can.

Don't have to cook anything and it will last for years."

"Well…" Stella looked in awe at the towering mountain of food that seemed hardly diminished even though they had both been packing it away steadily at their respective ends for the last ten minutes. "All this sure is going to come in handy on the *Dreadful*. So, maybe Sam's survival tendencies weren't such a bad thing after all. And what do you mean he left you? I thought you said he died."

"Before he died he left me." Millie looked at several jars of home-canned something that could either be light gravy or applesauce but had lost the labels. Then packed them into her container, anyway. "Went on a fling with some younger woman and only came back when he found out he was dying."

"Oh. I'm sorry."

"So was I. But I didn't have it in me to turn him away –not after being married twenty-two years. Look here – have you ever tried any of these?" She held up a tan package with black lettering on it. "They're MRE's. You know, military food rations."

"Not hardly. Where did you get so many?"

"From the Colonel. Said he could get more, too."

Stella stopped loading her containers and looked over at Millie. "I thought you said all this was Sam's idea. Oliver's only been here a little over a year, hasn't he?"

"It was Sam's idea to start with. But I'm a firm believer in taking care of myself during a national emergency. You think I'd be like some of those people you see on the news, just sitting around waiting for someone to rescue them? Some even dying? Not me. Not on your life! I'm going to be handing out help, not waiting for it. I never go to the store without bringing back a little something for my famine chest. Force of habit."

"I can see that. But Millie…" Stella straightened up for a moment and put a hand to her aching back. What a long week it had been! "It's obviously been more than could fit into a chest for years. Look at the size of this thing!" She looked up at the pile that nearly touched the ceiling in some places. "There's no way this is all going to fit into that galley pantry, even if Stuart does move all his paint stuff somewhere else. Shouldn't we prioritize?"

"Mason already built some water-tight crates so we could store the extra down in the hold. Believe me, we're going to need all of it when we find out there isn't a grocery store for a hundred miles up there and we get snowed in until spring in some frozen wilderness."

"Good grief, Millie!" Now, she couldn't help stealing the Colonel's phrase. "Doesn't that thought just send chills up your spine? Surely Mason wouldn't let us all get into such a--"

"He certainly would," her friend informed her. "Mason thinks he can survive anything and figures he can take care of half the rest of the world while he's at it. On account of he was in one of those prison camps during the Vietnam war."

"I didn't know that!" Stella stopped packing again, and looked back over at Millie; this time noticing she had split a seam on the side of her lavender colored pants from so much bending and stretching. "He doesn't seem the type."

"Nobody's that type, believe me. Don't let on to him I told you–he's real touchy about it. But you know what? It's because of that experience we ever met the Colonel.

On account of he wanted to use Mason's story in one of the chapters of his hero book. Mase got some kind of medal for something he did back then but I never could get him to show it to me."

"One of Oliver's heroes for a history book--I never would have dreamed! Isn't it rather amazing the way all of us have come together, Mil? I mean, it's almost like … like destiny, or something."

"It's destiny all right. Because while Mase figures it doesn't matter what condition that Alaskan lodge of his is in since we can live under a tree and survive off pine nuts if we have to. But he's going to be pretty darn glad I brought my famine chest along. Plenty of moose and salmon up there, he says. I say nobody wants to live off the same thing for eight months straight, no matter how much the stuff sells for down here in the states. He wouldn't last two weeks without hankering after a pot of my homemade chili, anyway."

"None of the rest of us would, either," Stella pointed out.

"So, get ready for the worst, is what I always say, then celebrate like crazy if nothing happens. Hey--do you realize what time it is, Stel?"

Stella glanced at her watch. "Why, it's three o'clock already, and I'm supposed to meet Oliver downtown at four! We have to get some last minute things for our cabin."

"Better take my car."

"But we might not be back until late."

"Doesn't matter. Mase is coming in to take the last of the stuff aboard and I'll be staying out there from now on. Everything of mine is in, already. Just make sure and lock up the garage when you bring it back, will you? The man who bought it won't be by until Saturday and Lou's picking up a swing shift tonight. Trying to get in all the hours she can before we sail."

"Thanks, Mil!" Stella missed the last words of instruction as she fairly flew up the cellar steps and into the basement.

One more flight of stairs in such a hurry only brought her to the kitchen, and she was already exhausted. How could she possibly clean up and get downtown in time? She certainly couldn't arrive in blue jeans, a checkered blouse and a babushka! Not that Oliver hadn't seen her in the worst of all possible conditions before. It was just that they were planning a farewell dinner at the *Luau Palace*, since they were practically still on their honeymoon.

Such a thoughtful man she had married… he never ceased to amaze her. Which is why she had no intentions of having him pacing the isles of the curtain department in a store down at the local mall because she completely lost track of time. She had enough shortcomings that would come out sooner or later, and had every intention of making the "honeymoon period" last as long as it possibly could.

So—in a snap decision—she heaved open the iron doors in front of the dumbwaiter and proceeded to climb in. If it had been a good enough elevator for Millie's invalid cousin Gerald all those years, it could certainly get her up to the third story without depleting every ounce of energy she had left. Except there was something in the way.

Several large items, wrapped with brown paper and string, that she could tell the minute she moved them, were paintings. But what were they doing here? Stella didn't have to wonder whether or not they were expensive because every original item in the old Hollywood retreat known as *Villa Nofre* had been worth a small fortune. Which is why—when curiosity got the better of her—she peeled back a corner of the top frame and peeked inside.

It was that ghastly modern art Millie said she detested, and had packed away into the attic, years ago. Worth a fortune on the right market, though, which she had also told her. Stella counted the frames. Seven of them. Probably the whole collection. Surely they should have been left in the attic with everything else up there for the family of the deceased owner to go through. That is…

Unless Millie had another plan of her own that none of the rest of them knew about.

The captain's quarters looked like an entirely different place than the day Stella had her first glimpse of it. Now there were brown plaid drapes at the windows to lend privacy and keep out cold drafts on chilly evenings (Stella loved plaids, they were so homey). A chocolate-colored Berber area rug had been tacked over the old oriental, and a frosted glass globe of Edwardian design (from which the boat actually had its origin) to replace the tasseled lampshade from the bootleg era. Not to mention every inch of the wooden walls had been scrubbed and oiled until they shown like honey.

Her book collection was in place (as if the shelves had been made to exact specifications!), and even the old stove—which now had a warm fire crackling away just to see how it would feel—had been newly blacked and polished over all its nickel trim. There was a new comforter set with matching pillows (browns and plaid) in a lovely little bedroom adjoining the quarters, too. They even had their own private bathroom with a shower.

It should have been heaven.

Instead, Stella sat on the couch (under her favorite rose-colored throw) beneath the Colonel's questioning gaze from where he sat behind the desk (with his writing things all around) and –for the first time– felt uncomfortable in his presence. She was amazed at how quickly she slipped back into her old ways. Like a puzzle piece locking into place, the practice of diverting confrontation by bringing up a shocking but less dangerous subject came as naturally as breathing to her. It always had. Yet, it was not having the same effect on her new husband as it had on the previous one.

"I don't believe it," he finally pronounced. "I just plain don't believe it."

"Do you regret all this then?"

"Stella, I would have married you if you were a hundred and three! Do you really think age has anything to do with it?" He rose up from the desk, unconsciously hiked up the back of his loose-fitting khaki pants, and began to pace.

In spite of the tense moment, she thought how all the rigors of the last few weeks were causing him to shed pounds, and wondered if he shouldn't buy a smaller size. "Looks are deceiving, Oliver. Especially these days." she went on.

"And that's the point!" He turned around just as she was putting the cap back on the coconut oil that had become a nightly ritual to rub onto her face. "Stella--" His tone was imploring. "You can't possibly sit there in those flowered silk pajamas, with that white, Chinese-collar robe thing that practically matches your hair, and expect me to believe you're eighty-one years old! It's ridiculous!"

"Longevity runs in my family."

"Hogwash! Even face lifts and Botox have to be disguised with fancy hairdos and make up. You haven't a thing under that oil but your natural skin."

"Must be the Swedish coming out in me," she mused. "Did I ever tell you my mother's family immigrated to Minnesota from Sweden, Oliver? Way back in… the late eighteen hundreds, I think it was."

He sighed and sat down at the desk, again, so heavily that the leather squeaked under the strain. "After all we've been through, Stel. It's disappointing you feel you have to hide anything from me."

"It isn't as if I made a conscious effort to hide it. It's just that the subject never came up. And now, only because you flipped through my passport."

"It was sitting right here on my desk, where Gerald dropped the mail this morning —both of ours came—I was just taking them out of the envelopes. Besides, that's not the point. I'm talking about whatever it is that's makes you feel it necessary to pass yourself off as someone twenty years older. I already said I don't believe the eighty-one-year-old bit. Not for a minute, I don't."

Stella didn't know what to say about that, so, she didn't say anything.

"Well, I'm sure you'll tell me the real story whenever you feel safe enough. Let's just let it go at that, my dear."

How odd that he should use the word, safe.

"I suppose it's this whirlwind romance of ours." She gave a relieved sigh at having barely avoided catastrophe. "Do you realize I know as little about you as you do me? A military career and you write hero books. That's all I know about you: outside of being divorced and having two grown-up sons you never see—they're so busy off in the military, themselves. Why, for all I know, you could be a… a former inmate of a mental institution."

"Oh, Stella – for crying out loud – don't you think I'd

have told you if there were something as serious as that in my past?"

"Not really."

"Well, I would."

Better not go there, then, as that serious omission might give him an even worse shock. Even though there was a perfectly acceptable explanation if she was ever allowed to explain. "People often try to get others to think differently of them than they actually are," she pointed out. "It doesn't always mean they're hiding something criminal. Take Mason, for instance."

She got to her feet and walked over to push back a shock of gray curls that had fallen onto his forehead. "He lets everyone assume he's nothing more than a self-centered, hard-drinking carpenter, and in reality, he won some sort of Medal of Honor he doesn't want anyone to know about. Imagine being ashamed of a Medal of Honor!"

"Soldiers often feel guilty if they happen to survive when so many of their comrades don't."

She settled comfortably onto his lap and he locked his arms around her waist.

Thank goodness! She didn't think she could stand it if there had been any true rift between them. "And look at Millie. All that fuss about Sam's memory and… they weren't even together until just before he died. He left her for a younger woman."

"Maybe she likes to forget the bad parts and remember it that way, herself."

"My point exactly, dear. Not to mention they were still married the whole time, so it wasn't exactly an untruth, either. Still, it all hit her terribly hard. No money of her own to fall back on. Did you know she spent years squirreling things away for hard times? And not just food, either."

"I take it you saw the famine chest."

"A famine chest I can understand—we should all have one. Hers is a monstrosity but I can understand it. But the art! Less than two weeks after J.D.--Mr. Willoughby, I mean—so graciously forgave her for selling off all that other stuff, too. There's no way she could be trading it in to pay electricity and repair bills, anymore. Where could she cash something that famous in where it wouldn't be found out? If I didn't know better, I'd say she had an entirely different plan for herself. One that doesn't include the rest of us. You know, I don't even think Gerald knows—and he's her cousin. Nobody does."

"What art?"

"All those famous modern art pictures I found in the dumbwaiter, this afternoon. The only reason I saw them is because I was late and needed a ride up instead of climb those hundreds of stairs. And there they were! All wrapped in brown paper and tied up with string—ready to mail. You don't do that just to move something to another room or leave in a closet. And they certainly aren't to decorate her cabin on the *Dreadful*, either."

"*Dreadnaught*, Stell. You know how it physically pains Stuart to hear you call it that."

"It's a much more fitting name, if you ask me."

"Try thinking about it as our gateway to adventure. By the time this trip is over, I'm sure we'll be almost as attached to it as Stuart is. Look how our Captain's quarters spruced up so well."

"Oh, they did! You know I was almost envious of

everyone else moving aboard before we did? I'm that fond of all this, already. I thought Millie was, too. She did tell me those pictures were worth a fortune, though. Then again, maybe she had second thoughts about leaving them in an empty house and decided to send them to the family directly. Do you think that's what it was?"

"That sounds a lot more like our Millie than absconding with them. Remember how upset she got at the prospect of going to jail? She probably just forgot about the paintings in all this confusion of moving. What do you want to bet she'll remember them halfway through Canada somewhere, and then fuss about it all the way to Alaska."

"You're probably right."

"We'll ask her."

"Which is entirely possible because we've all worked ourselves into a stupor this week, trying to keep up with Stuart. I wonder why the first thing we do, when anything doesn't seem quite right, is to think the absolute worst of people? I wouldn't be surprised if the whole thing turned out to be--"

The familiar strains of the Marine Band piped up from his shirt pocket, and Stella got up to put another log on the fire while he answered the phone.

"Henry, here. Oh, hello, Mason. Not back yet? No, just Stella and I. Villa looked all dark and locked up when we put the car back in the garage. Didn't even go in."

Stella stopped poking at the fire and turned around in time to see the Colonel's gray eyebrows scrunch together into his thinking expression. "Course we will. Be there as soon as we can."

She felt a tightening in her chest. "Now, what

happened?"

"Millie isn't at the house, and it's been over an hour since she was supposed to meet Mason there." He got to his feet and slipped the phone back into his pocket in one smooth motion. "Not answering her phone, either."

What could only be called a "wild goose chase" ensued. Stella threw some clothes on over her pajamas, and rode back across the bay with the Colonel and Stuart (who was driving all out), to search for Millie. By that time Mason was an exhausted wreck, having called every emergency room in town, thinking her heart condition may have got the better of her somewhere with all the stresses and strains of the move. Then he single-handedly began a search of all nooks and cupboards in the mansion from the attic down.

By the time the others arrived, he had reached the kitchen on the main level.

Stella forced herself not to think the worst and hurried off to search on her own. But what Millie had told her earlier about being stranded in the frozen north, hundreds of miles from grocery stores (maybe even electricity!), she certainly wouldn't blame her if she decided to go live back east with one of her children, after all. True, each of them had been sincere about sticking together. Especially after discovering what their individual prospects would be, should they all have to fend for themselves separately. All of them agreed they were more than capable of pooling their resources and living the same way they had here at the Villa, somewhere else. But Alaska!

To some place Mason had acquired in a card game, sight unseen.

Why, the only reason Stella wasn't quaking in her own boots, right now, was because it would be a grand adventure just getting there. Sort of an extended honeymoon. And if things turned out too badly, she and the Colonel still had enough money to rent something small to get by on. But the others didn't. And considering how attached they had all become she hadn't thought twice about not pitching in.

The truth was, pitching in for this little misfit family was beginning to change her life. It had brought her out of some of her own thin places and she had no desire to go back to those, again. She couldn't go back! Which was why she wanted to have a private talk with Millie, in case she really was thinking of desertion. They had to stick together!

If they didn't, the whole thing could turn into a disaster and nobody would succeed.

She was thinking of all these things as she headed down to the wine cellar (whether by premonition, or it was simply the last place she had seen Millie), and threw back the latch on the door. Even though it was impossible to accidently lock oneself inside and her friend could only have latched it if she had come out.

Which was exactly how Stella discovered an unconscious Millie, draped over a row of plastic bins, as if someone had conked her on the head. Something that proved false, as did a heart attack. In the end, it seemed the heavy door had somehow closed on its own, and –after realizing her cell phone wouldn't work in a place that could have doubled as a fallout shelter in case of World War III—she proceeded to console herself in the emergency liquor supply while waiting to be rescued.

Something that could happen to anybody, especially if they were claustrophobic.

Still, with one problem after another faced and solved by the increasingly brave band of adventurers, they did actually manage to sail out of the protected southern California bay, three days later.

It was a glorious spring day, the sea was calm, and the *Dreadnaught* behaved beautifully. So beautifully that the trip seemed charmed. So, it was no wonder, after ten days of worry-free voyaging (they even did several stints of night-traveling because the moon and stars were bright and spectacular), and only brief stops in San Francisco and Portland, they finally ended up anchored off Vancouver, Canada, to show their passports and wait for a border inspection to proceed north.

Captain Stuart did everything by the book. In fact, he had made this run several times in his working days (on more modern vessels but the course was the same), and left his little group of passengers to rest and relax on board while he collected all their passports and set out to take care of business. All of which went through without a hitch. Even during the long and thorough inspection. After that, a few hours of sight-seeing and the purchase of a few last-minute items, and they were soon on their way, again.

It was a very long way to Alaska.

However, the coast of British Columbia is a wild one, with long stretches of wilderness places, and weather that can change as fast as one's feelings. There were a few mornings they woke up enveloped by a thick fog (that Stuart referred to as a "pea souper"), and had to wait until it lifted to continue their journey. Something that had little effect on the happy group. Whether it was because of the marvelous sea air, or the fact they had enough supplies on board to get by for an entire year if they had to, no one knew.

Because, not only were they all getting along splendidly, they had become quite comfortable (and proficient) in their respective "sea duties." Even Stuart had to admit the voyage was turning out to be one of the best he had ever made. Mostly because of the food. With three women aboard who loved cooking, the meals were fabulous. He even started to contemplate the possibilities of taking on a few charters after this trip was over, in order to complete renovations.

But all that was before their first storm.

Up till that point, most of the travel had been motoring. Outside a time or two of raising the sails (in order to keep up skills, as Stuart put it), the entire trip, so far, had felt like nothing short of a delightful holiday cruise. For everybody.

Even Gerald, who took his "turn at the wheel" with the utmost seriousness and respect, was actually becoming dependable. He stayed precisely on course, did exactly what the Captain told him at all times, and was even getting a bit of color back into his face. Of course, he had to make a few concessions, considering his condition. He rarely left the main deck (where his cabin was situated), and—except for the few steps up to the wheelhouse—avoided stairs and companionway ladders, altogether.

He was cold most of the time, too, but solved that problem by wearing a black navy watch cap (both waking and sleeping), as well as half a multicolored Mexican poncho that was cut off at elbow-length so that he could still do his work. Something that made him resemble the haggard form of Lincoln, moving through hallways of the White House, during the last dark days of the Civil War. Without the beard, and should you come up on him from behind.

However, that part of sea—which funnels through the straits from the "big water" (as Stuart called it) outside the islands—can turn suddenly wild and dangerous with hardly any warning. And considering they had known nothing but idyllic conditions the entire way, all hands were caught horrifically unaware when one of those famous storms crashed into them. That is, all accept Captain Stuart.

Who knew exactly what to do in such conditions, if he only had at least one person who could lift more than fifty pounds in a full gale. He hoped everyone else could handle at least twenty and still manage to stay on their feet. This because the sea was so rough the engine propellers were out of the water half the time, and the old schooner was much more stable with her sails up than without them. After all, it was what she had been designed for.

Meanwhile, everyone except the Captain was seasick. Not counting the baby, who was never bothered by anything, and having a delightful time bouncing wildly, back and forth, in his "Johnny Jumper" attached to a cabin ceiling as he watched his "Uncle Gerald" throw up into a bucket. His mother and Mason were out on deck, doing their level-best at hauling the mainsail up, as Stella and Millie grappled with "taking up the slack" in the sheets.

This so Stuart could see to the sudden banging noises that were coming from his engine, and the Colonel—by sheer size and strength—struggled with the wheel to keep their ship bucking through the waves instead of getting trapped in the troughs between. All of which presented itself to Stella (even though she was scared-stiff, and wet to the bone in spite of rain-gear) as such a display of courage and cooperation that she would remember it for the rest of her life.

One particular scene, especially.

It was the expression on the Colonel's face (when she looked up at him through the wheelhouse window) after the mainsail suddenly tore in half and began flapping like thunder, causing the lines to go slack, and send them tumbling toward the rail when the boat began to roll. With the determination of a weight-lifter contending for Olympic gold, he clamped onto the wheel and began to inch the giant hull back up by brute force, in order to save them from shipwreck.

But it wasn't enough.

***

At the same time, down in the engine room, the Captain knew exactly what was happening, topside, by the way his vessel made the sudden roll to starboard and sent him crashing into the bulkhead. Now, they had it, he thought to himself, because not one of them up there knew what to do next. "Haul up that jib!" he hollered, even though no one could hear him from down there. "Get some way on before we lose her in this--"

BOOM! There was the loud bang of rigging as the boat wallowed over onto her other side, caught in the steep trough between waves. Which gave him a decision to make. Take the few minutes to replace the broken belt and get the engine going, again, or leave it to dash topside, and pull the foresails up so the boat would at least have enough steerage not to founder. "God help me!" he cried, heaving himself to his feet. "I'm at sea with a bunch of idiots!"

It was at that moment a dark form darted past him and he distinctly heard, "Fix the belt-- I got the sails!" in a tone of such confidence that his old Navy days kicked back in, and he found himself "snapping to" without so much as a care who it was.

He only knew he had a bona fide seaman aboard, after all, and a flood of relief washed over him. In the nick of time, too. Then it occurred to him he had never had such immediate attention from the Almighty in his entire life. Something which led to the disturbing conclusion that, either an angel had just passed by, or…

The *Dreadnaught* had gone down, already, and he was about to meet his maker.

6

A tumult of thoughts ran through Stella's mind during those moments. It wasn't the first time she had faced death, but it was the first time she had ever been able to stand up to that terror with such peace and utter clarity. What happened next played out before her in a sort of dreamlike slow motion, giving her plenty of time to react.

The first thing she did was to grab hold of Millie as she tumbled by, and pull her to the safety of the rail, where she could hold on. Then as the boat began to roll in the opposite direction, she felt the line she had dropped begin to whistle away over her feet, and picked it up. Just in time to wind it around a nearby cleat (why, she had never managed the task that fast before!) and stop the free-swinging boom from plowing into Mason, who had his back to it, trying to tie off from the other side. Disaster avoided. Almost like a miracle.

Which is just what she was thinking when she saw the dark stranger come running past her, right out onto the bowsprit that hung over all those wildly tossing waves. He peeled the canvas back with quick agility on yet another sail that was stashed there, and began hauling it up the stays. Only to be stopped by a tangle of tattered mainsail that had wound itself round the thick wire, about a third of the way up when the big one had torn loose.

"Lou!" called a familiar masculine voice. "Ninja ladder!"

The girl was beside him in an instant, and what Stella saw next was amazing.

He bent down long enough for her to climb up onto his shoulders and grab hold of the bunched up sail, in order to pull herself along the wire as he slowly stood up, again. Still standing on his shoulders when she reached the place the tattered pieces were wrapped around, he snatched a knife from his belt and handed it up to her.

The wire was attached at the top of the foremast, slanting down at an angle to the very tip of the bow. Another miracle. If the obstruction had been any higher, she wouldn't have been able to reach it. As it was she had the offending tatters cut away and was back on deck in a mere few moments.

At which point, Cole DeForio (Stella recognized him the minute Lou Edna climbed up and down over him with such confidence and familiarity), quickly finished hauling up the large jib sail, while Mason pulled the trailing line attached to it around a nearby winch-drum and tied it off. The boat immediately headed back up into the wind, and regained enough control for the Colonel to have steerage, again.

They were saved!

Less than five minutes after that the engine sputtered back to life, and the *Dreadnaught* continued to plow steadily through the storm toward the nearest harbor, where they could drop anchor and wait the thing out. A place not far off from Alert Bay (which was not on their list of official stops), and not a sign of civilization was in sight. But it was well protected and safe. And more welcoming to the exhausted adventurers than any waterfront town could have been.

The young couple disappeared almost immediately after they got there, giving everyone else time to collect themselves and their thoughts, down in the galley. They all needed to recuperate before the inevitable confrontation. At the very least, there was a lot of explaining to do.

"I take back every critical thing I've said about Shortcake," said Mason, holding one of the large mugs of hot bullion Millie was handing out to everyone who meandered in after changing into dry clothes. "Any girl who will hop-to like that in an emergency is all right by me."

"She lied to us, again, Mason." The Colonel was not one to give quarter to dishonesty. "Been hiding that young man, all along. Where--I have no idea--considering how thoroughly those officials went over this boat when we came through customs. Imagine what could happen if they had found a stowaway."

"I shudder to think about it," agreed Stella (another narrow escape!). She was sitting next to him at the table, wearing a matching knit hat and scarf (periwinkle blue), with her still-chilled hands hugging her own mug of bullion. Would she ever be truly warm, again?

"When you're in love you do crazy things," said Millie.

"When you're in love you aren't ashamed of it," Mason added. "So, he must be in some kind of trouble. Again."

"So..." The Colonel took a deep breath. "We've been

smuggling a criminal through Canada."

This just as Gerald dragged in, still somewhat wobbly, and so pale Millie immediately poured a large splash of brandy into his bullion before handing it to him. "Better sit down before you fall down, Gerry," she whispered.

"E-gads…" He sank onto the seat beside Stella. "Lou didn't bring any drugs aboard, did she?"

"Of course not!" huffed Millie. "She's too good a mother to get wrapped up in that stuff. Look how she quit drinking the minute she found out she was pregnant. And she's as loyal as my own daughter, too. In her own way."

"We could sit here guessing, all day." Mason got to his feet. "Let's get them in here and talk, so we can decide what's the best thing to do."

"Can't see as there is a best thing," said the Colonel. His cheeks were growing rosy from the warmth of the stove. Then again, he did have a bit more insulation than everyone else, with all those extra pounds turning to muscle, Stella mused. "Wouldn't be right to dump him off in a foreign country," he went on, "and he definitely did the right thing when he had to."

"Dump who off?" Gerald handed his empty mug back toward Millie (who had just bent down to re-twist the yellow towel she had wrapped around her wet hair), and knocked it out of his hand against her hip, instead. "Tell Stuart I need a little more time, Mil—I'm doing my level best!"

"Not you, Gerald. Our stowaway. Lou smuggled Cole DeForio, aboard, and now we're all accomplices." She snatched up the mug and refilled it, again.

"E-gads!" he replied, and took it.

At which point, Mason returned with the contrite young couple following behind, whose youthful good looks seemed absolutely striking in contrast to their bedraggled elders. Lou Edna's blonde hair was gathered into a band at the nape of her neck, she hadn't a speck of make-up on, and she was beautiful.

"Well, it was a snap decision," she began before anyone even asked them a question. "There were some bad people after him and I had no choice."

"One always has a choice," said the Colonel. "There are other ways to help besides breaking more laws."

"Let's get something straight, right off." Cole met the Colonel's gaze and pointed to his own chest for emphasis. "I wasn't the one who broke the law."

"Do you have a passport or don't you?" Mason asked him.

"To begin with I didn't break any laws," the young man corrected himself. "Like she said, it was a snap decision. I just didn't have enough time to get one."

"Bad people aren't usually interested in border regulations. What's Shortcake talking about, here?"

"It was me that talked him into it, Pop. I told him we could get good money at pawn shops for those pictures."

"What pictures?" asked Millie.

"The crazy art collection."

"What?"

"E-gads, Lou…" Gerald moaned. "The ones painted by E.J.'s first wife? They'd be worth a small fortune at *Christie's*, by now How much did you sell them for?"

"Nothing, they disappeared."

"After she spent the money they already gave us for a down payment, too." Cole wiped a trickle of water off the side of his face that was coming from his wet hair. "You don't cross those kind of people. They'll come after you for stealing peanuts."

"Those kind of people don't usually do payments," Mason said.

"They paid seven hundred and fifty dollars, based on the preliminary artist sketches," Lou informed them. "The ones in that portfolio. I needed some things for the trip if we're going to be gone so long. You know I spent a hundred and fifty just in diapers? Then baby food and— a bunny suit, of course. Three of them, in fact. The Senator's crawling around so much, now, he's got one wore out, already."

"Don't change the subject," said Mason. "We all know how money disappears."

Millie sat down on the other side of the table, next to Mason, with a heavy sigh. "You should have asked us, Lou. Those paintings weren't ours to sell. After everything J.D. did for us, too."

"But you said yourself they were garbage, Mil. And the whole place was going to be knocked down, anyway. I didn't think anybody would even notice."

"They weren't our things."

"Wrong's wrong, even if it helps you" quoted Gerald, before he got up to refill his mug, again. "You got taken on the sketches, too. They'd have brought a strong five thousand at auction."

"Yeah, well I don't happen to know any fancy art collectors," Cole pointed out. "And, by that time we were in a hurry."

"You're lucky you didn't let go of the paintings or we'd all be in a fix." Mason rubbed a hand over his unshaved chin. "Long as they're back at the house, we're safe. I'll deal with J.D. about the sketches. He's reasonable enough."

There was such a long silence that he glanced around the entire table. Now, everyone looked guilty. "They are at the *Villa*... right?"

"Pop..." Lou Edna shook her head in disbelief. "They just... disappeared! We looked everywhere for them!"

"What? Holy--" BOOM! His fist banged down with a resounding thump. "This whole situation's getting worse by the minute!"

"Hold on, Mase." The Colonel raised his hand to interrupt the outburst. "It just so happens Stella found them."

Such a unanimous exclamation of relief burst forth from everyone at the same time, it sounded staged. Except for Stella. She tried nudging the Colonel under the table but he spoke out too soon.

"I found them, all right," she finally confessed. "They were in the dumbwaiter."

"That's right where I hid them but they weren't there when we went back. Those guys were waiting for us and when we didn't show up, they kept calling. They said they were coming over to deal with us. We had to lock Millie in the cellar, too, because I just didn't have enough time to explain."

"You know I almost had a heart attack down there?" Millie accused. "I was in there for hours!"

"But you were out by the time we got back," the girl reasoned.

"A lot of this is my fault, "said Stella. "You see, I had a bit of extra time before we moved onto the boat and mailed them off to the pawn shop they were addressed to. As a favor to Millie because her return address was on there."

Now, a unanimous gasp of horror escaped everybody.

"My pills!" Millie reached into the pocket of her pink housecoat, in search of them. "My heart pills! Oh, Mase—I'm going to faint!"

"Wait!" This time, it was Lou Edna who raised her hand. "It's OK—it's OK! Oh, this is all too funny!" She leaned her head back to indulge in a moment of nervous laughter. "If you mailed them just the way they were, we're OK!"

"You have the weirdest sense of humor, Lou." Cole got up and poured himself a cup of coffee, realized it wasn't coffee, and poured it down the sink, instead. "I've never felt this stupid in my life and we still have major problems, here."

"J.D.'s going to be wondering where those pictures are!" Millie complained. "I gave him our forwarding address, too." She moaned at her own stupidity. "Now, when they turn up on the black market somewhere, any investigator with half a brain will be able to trace things back to me. The real crooks will get away, scot-free, and I could end up in women's prison, after all! Lou—how could you do this to me!"

"I didn't do anything that bad, Millie. I addressed them to *Peabody's Peculiar Treasures*—J.D.'s antique place—not the pawn shop we were dealing with. In case you found them in the dumbwaiter before we could actually make the deal. Didn't want to give you another heart attack."

"You mean, I didn't send them to the mafia, after all?"

Stella was so relieved she leaned her forehead against the Colonel's shoulder and sighed. "Oh, thank heaven!"

"Mr. Peabody's probably had them for days, now," the girl assured. "So—other than harboring an illegal allien--"

"Oh, Lou Edna!" Millie dropped her face into her hands. "If you aren't the death of me one of these days, I will be a lucky woman!"

"Shortcake, we can handle." Mason jerked a thumb toward Cole. "It's him we got to figure out what to do with, now."

"I'll tell you what we're gonna do with him!" The booming voice of Captain Stuart echoed from the companionway leading down to the engine room. He ducked smartly into the galley, with his hair all slicked back, and a clean shirt on. It had a small rip at the left shoulder, and only smelled faintly of diesel.

"Yeah, I knew this was coming sooner, or later, so…" Cole stood up straighter and looked him in the eye. "Let's have it, Old Man."

"You're promoted to First Mate."

"Are you kidding me?"

"You will remain aboard this vessel—without shore leave—all the way to Alaska. Where you will immediately apply for a passport. And the rest of you…" Stuart looked them all over with a warm appreciation shinning in his eyes, and pronounced, "Are hereby released from idiot-status. By the Almighty—you performed like regular sailors, out there. Every last one of you!"

That night, as Stella sat tucked beneath her rose-colored throw reading before a pleasantly crackling fire, it suddenly occurred to her how far they had all come, working together as a team. Why it had literally saved them! And—without the many miracles she was so sure she had experienced that day—they could all be dead. In fact, she was beginning to feel like something of a cat with nine lives, lately, the way she had been escaping so many disasters.

Now, here she was in her safe little home, in this quiet harbor, halfway to Alaska. Could it be that God truly cared for her—in a personal way—and took a "divine hand" in all things concerning her? Why, if that were true… a person could do just about anything. An ordinary person would be capable of doing extraordinary things.

Maybe even great things.

All at once, an incredible sense of peace and contentment settled over her. She wondered if it wasn't truly the most wonderful feeling she had ever experienced. What's more, for the first time in her entire life, she had someone to share it with. A person who understood such things. She looked over to where the Colonel was working away contentedly on his next book of heroes.

"Oliver?"

"Yes, my dear?" he replied without looking up right away. Stella loved it when he got involved in his work. His face went through so many different expressions it was almost like watching a movie.

"I just thought you might like to know something."

He looked over at her then. "Yes?"

"I'm sixty-three."

"I thought so, Stel. You know that's just what I thought? It's a wonder they don't ask you to prove it whenever you renew your driver's license. It really is."

"When you have white hair, that's all anyone really notices about you."

"Hmm." He drummed his fingers lightly on the arm of his chair, as if thinking. "Anything else you want to tell me about all that?"

"Not at the moment." There would be plenty of time to tell him about those other things. She would tell him little by little. And—who knows—in the telling, maybe she would have more of this peace and contentment to fill her life. And less of those visions like that lady standing at the stove. Where did such things come from?

"You know, my dear…" He suddenly closed down his laptop and gave her his full attention. "Everyone has something to hide. Every last one of us. Look at Cole and Lou Edna. The lengths they went to pull this whole thing off. And all for seven-hundred and fifty dollars, that made them feel worthless inside."

"You have to admit it was clever the way they managed it, though," she said. Stella knew what it was like to be forced into desperate decisions and then end up in a worse place because of them. "Her dropping him off in the rowboat on the American side, late at night when we were all asleep, and then bringing him over the next night, again, after the inspection. He's been aboard all this time, and not a one of us had a clue."

"Yes, and if they would put that much effort toward honest work, they'd have more than enough respect to live on by now. Along with everything else that comes from doing what's right."

"Maybe they will, after all this." Stella closed her book and smiled. "He was certainly surprised when he got promoted to First Mate! Did you see the look on his face? It was like that was the first decent thing anybody ever did for him in his entire life."

"Wouldn't be surprised if it was. For sure he'll turn out to be the best hand Stuart's ever had. Wait and see."

"I hope so."

"They'll have a strong bond between them, too. I could see it's begun already. It's what comes of sharing something of yourself that gets met with acceptance and fair judgment from others. On the other hand, hidden things eat away at you a bit at a time, over a long period of time. It's one of the best forms of destruction there is."

Stella thought that was probably a good lead-in to tell him her own story. But it had been such a long and trying day. An extreme of highs and lows. The Colonel was right, of course. She knew it in her heart as soon as he said those words. But just as she was contemplating whether or not she was even up to such an ordeal, he smiled that wonderful smile of his.

"No need to speak of it any more, tonight, Stel. We have all the time in the world." He answered the question as if she had spoken it out loud. "Besides that, we start with ourselves. Just put ourselves in God's hands, and let him reveal what we need to change, a bit at a time. Somewhere along the line we become more transparent with everyone else, too. And one day we may just wake up and realize we are actually starting to resemble God, Himself. 'From glory to glory,' as the scriptures tell us. Just by watching what He does for us every day. Looking for it, even."

"Sounds wonderful when you put it that way, Oliver. Changing for the better, I mean."

"It's a miracle, my dear… an out and out miracle!"

***

Benjamin Franklin, who was quoted at the beginning of this story, was a man who threw in his lot with others, against impossible odds, many different times during his life.

Difficulties that were overcome not so much because he was a good businessman, an avid scientist and inventor, or even an amazing diplomat. But because, as he said, "Our prayers, Sir, were heard, and they were graciously answered. All of us who were engaged in the struggle must have observed frequent instances of a Superintending providence in our favor."

I find it interesting during research, to discover how much those who do great things seemed to have been "divinely prepared" beforehand. Benjamin Franklin is a good example of this. Even though he was born into a large working-class family (one of the youngest of 17 children), and had to be apprenticed into a trade at the age of twelve, he was raised by Puritan parents, and eventually settled in Philadelphia: that productive "experimental city" established under the Quaker influence of William Penn. The "city of brotherly love."

I also found it interesting that Franklin did his most important—and most difficult—work after the age of seventy. In his famous autobiography, he put together a list of personal "virtues" he lived by that he felt were vital to his success, especially in working with others. You can find this short, easy-to-read ebook, for free, via the following link.

I feel richer for having read it, myself.

http://www.gutenberg.org/files/36151/36151-h/36151-h.htm

THE PUSHOVER PLOT

A Stella Madison Caper

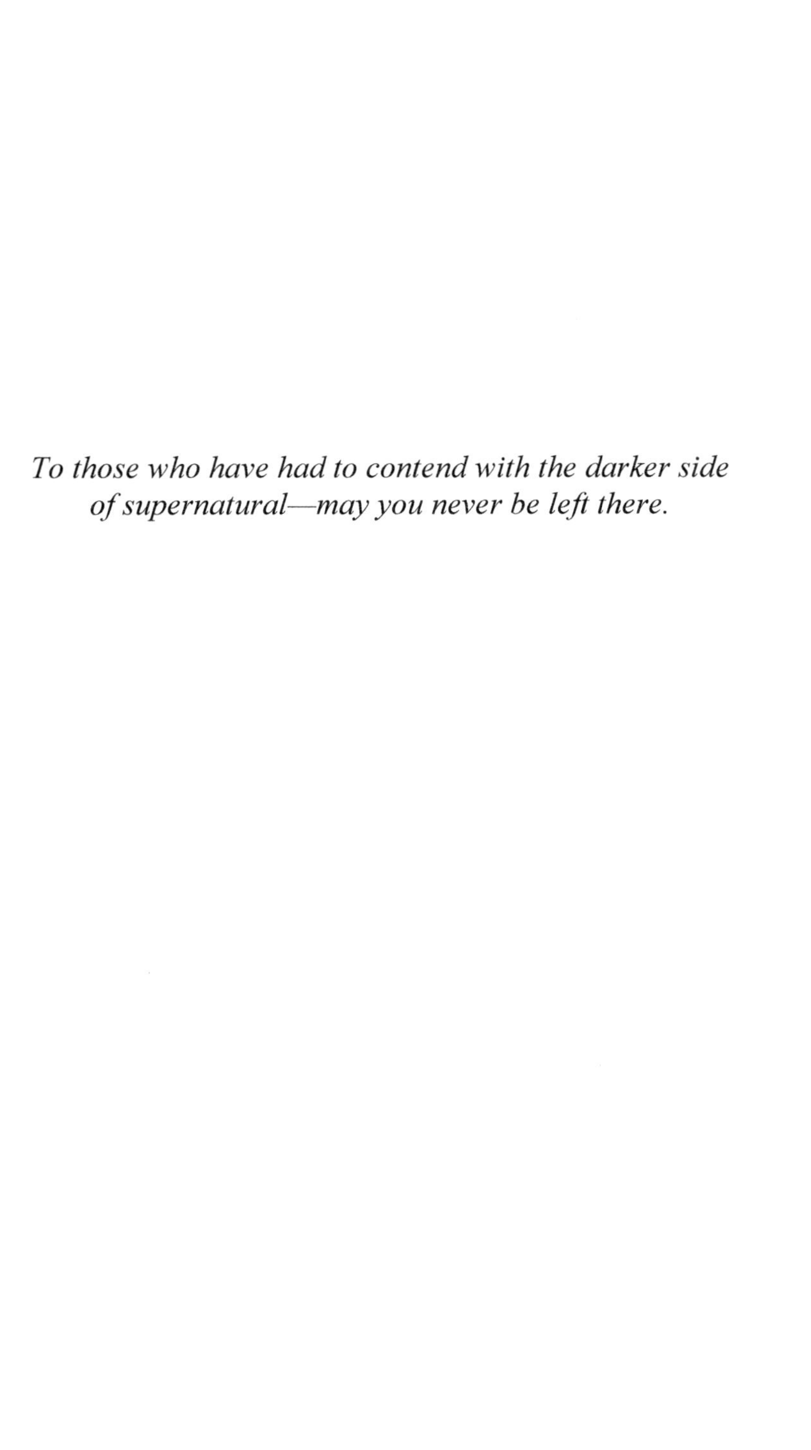

To those who have had to contend with the darker side of supernatural—may you never be left there.

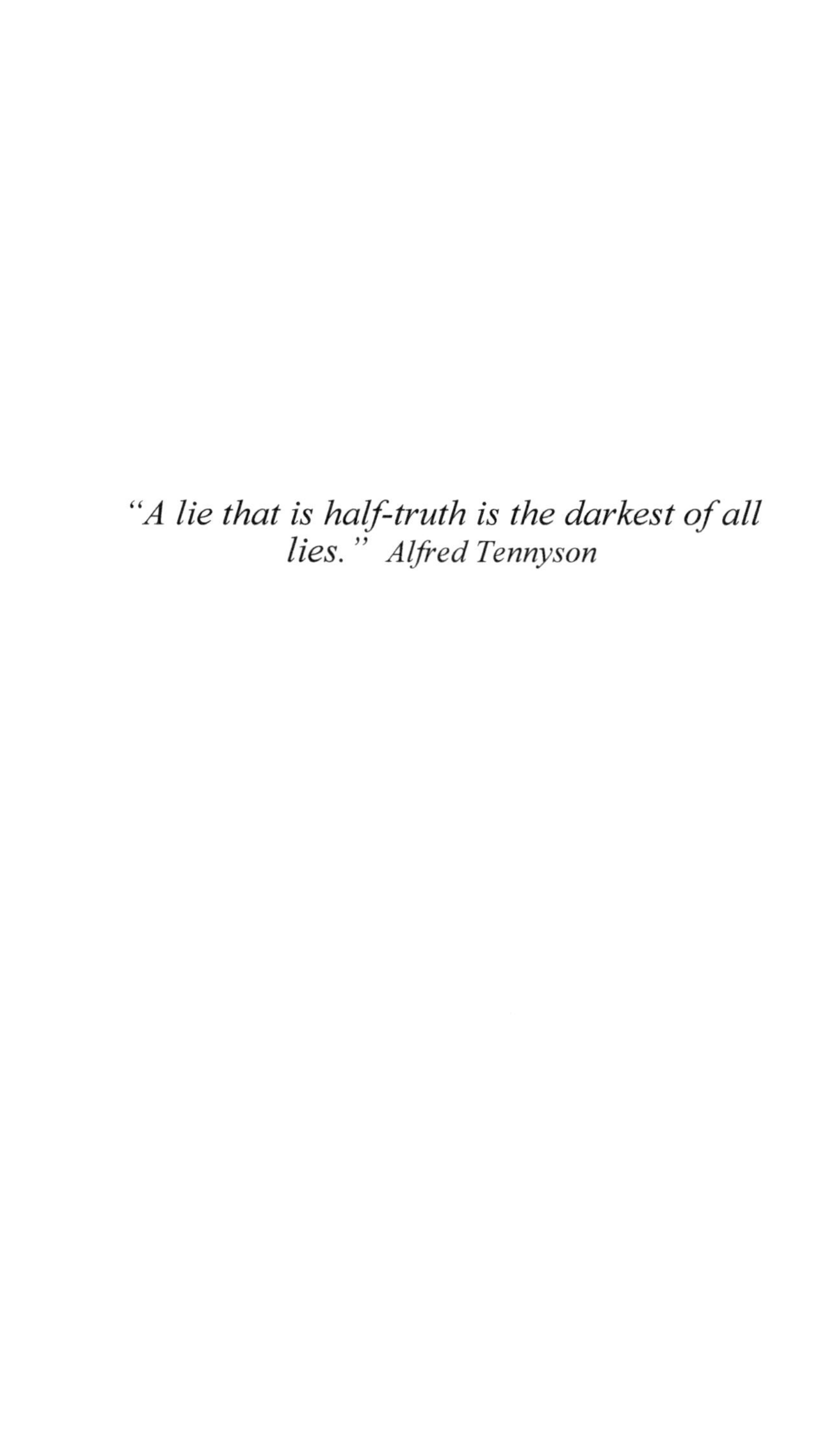

"A lie that is half-truth is the darkest of all lies." Alfred Tennyson

Stella Madison walked down the long dark hallway and deliberately ignored the flutter of fear it gave her. It was ridiculous, really, considering how many others were nearby who wouldn't hesitate to respond to any call for help. Then a regular jolt replaced that flutter because she suddenly remembered how often her own fears had robbed her of her voice in the most desperate hours. Something which made her revert to the old childhood trick of darting from safety to safety as fast as she possibly could.

So, having left the warm comfort at the side of her sleeping husband, she veered toward what had originally been known as the First Mate's cabin, to listen for the deep, reassuring snores of Mason Jeffries. Then to the faint sliver of light shining beneath Gerald's door (who still slept with a light on to "orient himself" even though they had all been aboard the *Dreadnaught* for nearly a month). After that, it was only a hop and a skip to the galley, where Millie left a light on over the stove in case anyone should get hungry in the middle of the night and come looking for a snack.

In fact, she began to hear somebody moving around in there as she got closer, along with the distinctly delicious smell of *Ovaltine* (why, she hadn't tasted any of that in years!). Evidence that someone beside herself hadn't been able to sleep, either. How nice it would be to enjoy a quiet chat instead of wading through the predawn hour all alone. Millie needing to take one of her pills, maybe, or Lou, up with the baby for some reason. Although if it was Captain Stuart, she probably wouldn't stay long as he was about the oddest person she had ever known. Not counting mentally deranged people which she had seen more than her share of.

Funny how memories from so long ago came suddenly to mind at certain times.

"I guess I'm not the only one who couldn't sleep," she spoke quietly as she pushed through the door, so as not to startle whoever it was. Only no one answered. Instead, she caught just a glimpse of someone disappearing through the companionway door on the far side of the sailboat's galley that led down to below decks. Someone in a full-length, light-colored gown and a dark braid that hung halfway down their back.

Stella got goosebumps when she saw that because none of the *Dreadnaught's* crew had hair that long. She reached for the corner of the large iron stove to steady herself but got even more of a fright to discover it was stone cold. No one had been heating any hot chocolate in here. Maybe it had been another stowaway. Considering all the dark nooks and crannies in this vessel and how many weeks Lou Edna had managed to hide her young man without a one of them having the slightest idea... it was a possibility.

A better one than the alternative, anyway.

Besides, how could those terrible things be happening, again, when she was cured of all that so long ago? Especially when her wonderful new life had just begun. They couldn't be! There simply had to be another explanation. She pulled open the narrow cupboard next to the stove where they kept all the hot drink supplies, and began to rummage through. Teas, coffee, hot cider, bouillon, hot chocolate... but no *Ovaltine.* That distinct mixture of malt in it was unmistakable. A realization that turned the cozy galley intimidating and made her want nothing more than to hurry back to where she belonged.

Along with another urge to have that talk with the colonel about her not-so-ordinary past that she kept putting off. In a few quick steps she was pushing back through the door, again, but only to collide with what looked like an old woman wrapped in a shawl, fairly gliding down the shadowy companionway.

At the same time Stella toppled backward, a distinctly male voice hollered, "Away, you foul spirit!" before tripping right over the top of her and landing hard on the other side. Along with an empty mug and sauce pan that clattered across the floorboards. "What—what? Good grief! Stella! Is it really you?"

"Of course, it's me! That's an awful thing to call someone, Gerry."

"What are you—doing—wandering around this time of night in that—that whatever it is?"

"It's my white terry with a Chinese collar." She got to her feet, feeling rather silly now that someone else was there. "I'm not going to say what I thought you were, with that cut-in-half serape you always wear on top of everything."

"I detest being cold, and the rest got in the way of my arms." He took the hand she offered, to get himself up off the floor. "Sorry for the name-calling. But—blast!" It was part of a Captain Stuart phrase (after a month at sea, they were all talking like old salts), "You scared the daylights out of me! Took you for another one of those ghastly apparitions."

"You mean, you actually saw one?"

"One? They're all over the place around here. Getting so a man can't even hot up his *Ovaltine* without running into the things."

So, she did smell *Ovaltine*! Stella laughed out of sheer relief. "You don't know how glad I am to hear that. But the stove's cold, how did you do it?"

"Have a hotplate in my room but no sink. And I don't find anything in the least funny about it. All this rot, it's —it's serious business." He pushed the black watch-cap farther back on his head and then picked up his dishes. "Makes me rue the day I ever went gallivanting after such stuff. If I only knew then what I know now!"

"I'm sorry, Gerry. I wasn't making fun. I just had sort of a scare, myself. I'm glad it was you I ran into and not... something else."

"Yes, well... I must say, it's things like this that made it necessary to switch my major to botany from Medieval history, if you want to know the truth."

"I thought you told me your degree was in archeology." They went back through the cabinway door into the galley. "Even said you taught a few semesters of it at the junior level. Remember?"

"Yes, of course. It's how I originally landed a contract from the private school I worked at for so long. When a position opened up in the biology department, I jumped at the chance to get out of it and back into botany, again. Especially since I was working on my master's by the time."

"Oh. I thought you said you were working on a master's in archeology."

"I was, originally. However, it was worse than the Medieval, what with all those curs-ed artifacts we were forever digging up. Didn't like it at all after I'd finished. And the thought of spending so many hours in dusty museum basements, cleaning and cataloging them... well, they were as bad as the castles—worse even. Then, again, it might have just been me. Now, I actually think the things followed me over from England. That's where I first opened the door to them, anyway."

"The apparitions?"

"Seems like it. I tell you, that whole castle study was a nightmare. Never even finished out the class."

"I don't blame you. There's nothing worse than being scared out of your wits." Then she corrected herself. "Other than being dead, altogether."

"Sometimes I think I might as well be, the way it's ruined my life." He turned on the water at the sink in the far corner to rinse out his things, and the soft whir of the water pump went on. "Oh, and that bosh about them not being able to travel over water? Isn't true. Not one bit. It's been ten times worse since I came home."

"You mean, you're not Millie's cousin from England? Then why do you talk that way?" Stella was beginning to wonder if Gerald might be one of those compulsive liars, that you couldn't believe a word from. Or, a mentally unstable type that could have been helped in hospitals but never qualified for the programs because they weren't dangerous. The kind more easily controlled with medication. He did take an unbelievable amount of pills every day.

"Oh, we're cousins, all right. Born and raised in the same town. But it's a... well, it's a fake accent." He glanced over at her with a slight apologetic smile, just enough to show the space between his two front teeth. "Started when I went to college. You know, to impress people. Now, I can't quit."

"It's more old English than modern, you know. I keep expecting you to burst out with "forsooth!" or something."

"Or, dastardly," he added, "It's true, I do like the old phrases best. Always have. I like to think I was born out of time, except—with the high infant mortality back then —I probably wouldn't have made it past the age of three. Rate I'm going, now isn't much better, though. Putting up with all this when I'm hardly past fifty."

"You attribute some of your physical ailments to these...um... apparitions, too?"

"Mostly. The shaking, the weakness, insomnia... that sort of thing."

Stella gave a thoughtful sigh and sat down on the tufted burgundy cushions (that were a bit threadbare and oil-stained) surrounding the dining area. "I've been seeing an apparition, too, Gerry," she suddenly confessed. "I thought it was all in my mind. Hallucinations, or something. But two people can't both be having the same hallucinations. Right?"

"Highly unlikely." He came over to sit across from her, still drying his hands on a blue dishtowel. "What have you been doing to get rid of yours? We should compare notes."

"I never knew you could get rid of them. I thought they just happened."

"Of course you can get rid of them. Or, so I've heard. There's a whole theological philosophy about that. Haven't had any luck with it, myself, yet, but I've only just started trying. Meanwhile, mind telling me how you cope?"

"Cope with what?"

"How you deal with it all. You know, the ugliness, the torment, and—"

"The what?"

"And the out-and-out filth!"

"Good heavens!" She shuddered at the very thought. "I haven't seen anything as terrible as all that! Only a lovely middle-aged woman from some bygone era. And only a couple of times."

"Then I must caution you to be careful," he warned. "They never stay lovely for long."

Stella woke up the next morning to the smell of freshly brewed coffee and the humming of the engine as it chugged along underneath them. By the way the sunlight was shining in through the porthole beside the bed, she could tell it had to be at least eight-o'clock, already. She had overslept. Either that or she was reluctant to leave the cozy comfort of her bed after a night like the last.

She was determined to have that talk with the colonel, sometime today. No matter what.

But not during his writing time. He put so much into his work she didn't have the heart to distract him with anything else before he finished his "daily stint." She had always been in awe of writers. How they could chronicle things in a way that made you feel you were actually living through the period, yourself; or even create another world, entirely. She fully believed reading good books had saved her from some of the darkest times in her life. It was also why she now had a collection of thousands.

"You're missing some beautiful scenery, dearest." The colonel popped in with his usual cheerfulness just long enough to set a steaming mug down on the built-in nightstand. "We even have fresh cinnamon rolls, this morning. Seems our Millie has been out-doing herself in the baking department, again."

"I think it takes her mind off leaving everything she's ever known and a kitchen is her most comfortable place." Stella sat up and plumped her pillow into a better position to lean against. "Thank you, dear. I'll be right out and we can enjoy the view together."

She threw on a pair of jeans and a navy knit sweater, then ran a quick brush through her hair. Knowing it would be a long trip she had it cut a bit shorter before she left. A month later and it seemed just right to turn under in the usual manner with her touch of natural curl.

Stella's hair had gone prematurely white (which she had several theories about). But thinking of it just now, she realized having white hair was the only thing that could have allowed her to do what she had been forced to do all those years, ago. So, looking at it in the perspective of her spiritual awakening, she could see how it had actually been providential.

That perhaps God had been looking after her even when she didn't know he was. What a comforting thought! If—in the times when she didn't know how to call out to him—he had dropped life-saving information and coincidences into her path in spite of herself.

Oliver already had their wooden tray set up in the middle of the couch (or settee, as it was called in nautical terms) when she joined him. That way, they could each sit at either end, and watch the beautiful scenery slip away behind them through the bank of French windows above it.

"Ready for a refill?" he asked, taking up the silver and glass French press they made coffee in every morning, here in their quarters. It had become customary for everyone to fend for themselves for breakfast and lunch to accommodate individual ship-board duties (as Captain Stuart called them). But they all gathered for family dinners each night.

"Just a warm-up," she replied. "I still have half a cup. Didn't want to miss any of the show."

"And what a show it is, this morning. See how close we're traveling between these two rocky islands? Look how the water is so still our wake is nothing more than a wide ripple in the shape of a V spreading out behind us."

"It's the most beautiful place I've ever seen in my life."

"Absolutely magnificent!"

"And those tall sun-warmed pines—I could smell them wafting in through the open porthole. It was just glorious. Made me think back to summer camp days when I was growing up. Funny how things of nature impress you so much more in your youth."

The colonel glanced over at her with a mild surprise —he had one of the most expressive faces she had ever seen. Sometimes, she was sure she could tell exactly what he was feeling without him having to say a single word. Especially when he was working away at his writing. Now, a glint of delighted enthusiasm came into his gray eyes and she was sure he had hit on a break-through, or conquered some road-block in his current manuscript this morning.

"Interesting you should bring that up, Stel! Because I was having the very same thoughts, myself, this morning. Young people being so impressionable, and all."

"Isn't that amazing. Only married a month and already we're starting to think the same thoughts. What brought it on?"

"A bit of inspiration that dropped into my mind and fit like a glove." He set his coffee down, put his hands on his knees with a decisive smack, and said, "My dear, I have decided to write a book for boys!"

Another coincidence! Wasn't she thinking about important information being "dropped down" at vital times only a few minutes ago? Oliver had called it an inspiration, and simply taken it in stride. If it truly was a piece of information from heaven—designed especially for them—what a wonderful way to live that would be! At least, that's how Stella was thinking about it just then.

"Are you talking about one of your hero books scaled down to a reading level for younger people? Why, Oliver, I think that would be marvelous." She cut a piece of cinnamon roll off with her fork and popped in in her mouth. "Mmm. Light, perfectly spiced, with just a touch of almond flavor in the glaze."

"I don't think they can get any closer to perfect."

"No doubt. But back to heroes. Your stories are so good. Even more so because they're true. I don't think children get enough truth these days. In fact none of us do. When I taught school it seemed like so much that was offered to young people was beneath them."

She paused for a moment, wondering, hit on a bit of logic that seemed to fit, then continued her thinking out loud. "I remember there was some new philosophy going around that students had short attention spans. But you know something? Maybe they were simply bored by things that really didn't have any depth. And, Oliver?"

"Yes, keep going—I like how our thoughts keep running in the same directions."

"Well, I think boys would find stories about heroes anything but boring. Or even too difficult. In fact, I believe they would rise to it."

"That's exactly it, Stell—they will rise to it! Only I'm not going to write them a story about heroes. I'm going to write one that will show them how to become one." Then he threw back his silver-haired head and laughed at the sheer pleasure of the thought. It was so delightful and catching Stella couldn't help laughing with him.

"And I know just how to do it, too!" he declared. "Because I know boys like the back of my own hand!"

At ten o'clock, Stella went into the galley to get a start on the lasagna she would be making for dinner. The place wasn't half as scary in the daytime. Especially with everyone coming through on various errands or simply to get a bit of something to nibble on. There was a large porthole over the sink where one could look out while chopping vegetables or doing dishes, and today it was so lovely it practically took her breath away.

They were moving through a place called Johnstone Strait, after some particularly tricky maneuvering through another place called the Seymour Narrows. They had to leave an hour earlier than the usual schedule in order to catch the narrows at slack tide. But Captain Stuart knew his stuff—he had even taken this route once before. Of course that was many years ago, and he had been driving a tugboat back then. Hauling shipping containers full of all manner of merchandise and personal effects bound for Alaska.

Now, the danger was past and the waterway had opened up into a long, wide channel of lovely pine-forested islands, with little coves and harbors to pull into. Should anyone take a fancy to do that. However, the crew of the *Dreadnaught* had fallen into the comfortable routine of setting out at seven each morning (if there wasn't a fog), and then being settled at anchor somewhere else between six or seven in the evening. Which was always daylight this time of year because the sun rose somewhere around five-thirty, and didn't disappear until after nine in these northern latitudes.

Stella was thinking about all these things when Cole DeForio (that handsome young man Lou Edna had smuggled aboard when they first left California, and had now become their much-appreciated First Mate) came in looking for Millie. It wasn't until she looked up from scattering freshly-grated Parmesan cheese over her second layer to tell him Millie was taking a nap, that she noticed he had the Senator tucked under one arm as if he were a football instead than a baby.

"Oh, good heavens, Cole..." She wiped her hands on her apron and reached for the toddler. "That's no way to--"

But the boy was having the time of his life (such a good-natured baby!) and gave her a big grin when she turned him right-side up, again.

"I don't know anything about babies," the young man replied. "Only bringing him to Lou or Millie so Gerald can take his turn at the wheel."

"Nonsense." Stella couldn't help reverting to her teacher-tone at such a remark. "I can tell you everything you need to know about them in two sentences. They're just little people. Give them the same respect you would anyone else and they'll love you forever."

"Kid doesn't even talk, Mrs. H, what's to respect?"

Cole had a beautiful smile to set off his dark hair and rugged handsomeness and he must have known it. Because Stella had never seen anyone who had so perfected the art of charming others. In spite of which she was completely taken in by him, herself. Then again, she had always had a soft spot for the restless types, especially when their hearts held the least bit of sensitivity toward others. Which this young man's did. Not to mention the unashamed gratefulness he carried for Captain Stuart, who promoted him to First Mate status rather than sending him to jail.

"The same things you respect in any other person," she replied. "Like holding him right-side up, for starters. Then look him in the eye and call him by his name."

"Senator's no name for a regular person—especially a squirt like that." He reached a muscular forearm in front of her (that sported a tattoo of a ship's anchor), to snatch some of the Parmesan she had been grating. "I don't know what Lou was thinking to name him that. Isn't going to make things better for him, only worse."

"I'm inclined to agree with you but it wasn't our decision."

"Do you call him Senny, or Torry? I don't like either."

"Call him anything you want, as long as it's nice. That's what I do." Then, by way of demonstration, she held the child up until his darling little face was on a level with her her own, smiled her friendliest smile, and said, "Hi, Sonny Boy! Would you like a cracker?"

To which he gave a delighted squeal and nearly bounced out of her arms in anticipation.

Cole laughed at the obvious answer and ruffled the baby's dark curls. "OK. I get it. Mind keeping him a while? Lou and I had some... uh...words, last night. We need to talk."

"I'd be happy to. I'll put him in his high chair and give

him a snack."

Which was exactly what Stella was busy doing when he was back not five minutes after he disappeared down the companionway steps, as if there was a fire in the engine room, or something.

"We gotta turn the boat around!" He was headed for the wheelhouse, on his way out the other door that led to the decks. "Lou's Gone!"

After that, a near panic ensued.

No one objected to turning around—of course they would turn around—but what had gotten into the girl? She left the ship without permission. Something that was a near sin, in Captain Stuart's estimation. Besides that, he informed them all, it was no small thing to turn around. This because they couldn't just chug back through Seymour Narrows without waiting for the tide to turn.

"Why can't we shove it full throttle and push right on through, Stuart?" Gerald had lost all color in his face at the news and was shaking with worry as he turned the wheel over to more capable hands. "Blast! It's an emergency!"

"Because of the blasted nineteen-knot current roaring through there about now, Gerald. We only do ten. When she's in top condition." The Captain checked fore and aft, to make sure there were no other nearby vessels, then gave the wheel an expert spin to start the turn.

He didn't look like a captain should, with that mop of gray hair sticking out in all directions, and those bushy black eyebrows that nearly made a strait line across his forehead when he squinted his eyes to look at something. And he didn't dress like one, either. But Stella had to admit his threadbare (oversized) black sweater, faded jeans, and tennis shoes with no socks, did not seem to effect his expertise in handling his own boat.

"Oh, that girl's going to be the death of me!" Millie sank down onto one of two deck chairs that were at either end of the wheelhouse. The left side of her auburn twist was falling out of the hair-clip, since she had been roused from her nap.

All seven of them were crowded into the small enclosure, not counting the Senator, who was seated comfortably on Stella's hip, avidly watching the drama unfold, and mirroring each speaker's expression as they spoke.

"It's not like Shortcake to up and leave without saying anything." Mason pushed his fisherman's cap farther back on his head and ran a thoughtless hand over the three-day stubble on his chin. "She lies ninety percent of the time about where she's going but she always tells us she's going."

"Did anyone mention to her we were leaving early this morning?" Even the colonel had left his desk to see what was happening. "I thought I heard somebody on deck around five-thirty, just after I started work. But I assumed it was Stuart, or Cole, getting things ready for departure."

"Where on earth would she be going at five-thirty in the morning?" Stella wondered out loud.

The question caused a heavy silence to fall over the group until, one by one, all eyes finally settled on Cole. He was leaning against the chart table in the back corner, his troubled face in a turmoil as to whether or not he was going to tell everything he knew. His gaze met Stella's and he took a deep breath. She had been silently willing him to speak up and he read the message as if she said it right to him. However, rather than explain, he simply pulled a folded piece of note paper out of his back pocket and handed it over to Millie.

Dear Family,

I am not fit to be a decent mother or anything else. Please take good care of my boy.

Lou

At which point Millie burst into tears, and the baby right after.

"She's a deuce of a good mother!" Gerald smacked a fist into his palm as if it might somehow help him think. "It's the only thing she is good at!"

"A good mother doesn't desert her own child, no matter what the circumstances," The colonel intoned. And looking up at him from the side, with that rather Grecian profile and wavy silver hair, Stella thought how he resembled one of those ancient prophets whose word was always law. Then, again, he never did have much patience for Lou Edna and all her lies.

"Oh, why do all my children end up leaving me?" Millie choked back a sob to ask. "What's wrong with me? I feel like I'm infected with some kind of curse on families!"

"Millie, that's not true," Stella objected, bouncing the baby in a soothing motion and trying to comfort her former landlady at the same time. "Why you've got a bigger heart for families than any person I know. Just look at all the people you're family to that aren't even related to you." She didn't mention that she wasn't related to Lou Edna, either, but it didn't seem the time.

"Thank you, Stella," Millie sniffed and reached into the pocket of her sweater for a tissue. "It's just you have to wonder when all this love you feel keeps chasing people away."

"We can philosophize, later," said Mason. "Right now, I'm thinking Campbell River is a devil of a big place, and not a one of us here—except Cole—is of an age to be raising another kid. At the very least, we're gonna have to split up just to cover enough ground for a look-see. Then reconnoiter."

Now, Cole straitened to his full height and declared, "I'll find her if I have to—"

"You, mister," said the Captain, in no uncertain terms, "are an illegal alien in this country and will stay aboard ship. Be prepared to fire up the engine in one big hurry, though, in case we have to drag her back kicking and hollering."

"But, Cap, I—"

"No buts. We can't afford the local laws in on this mess. By the hoagie! Do we even have a birth certificate on this kid? They don't take kindly to people dragging other people's kids across borders around here."

A statement which produced another grave silence.

"Mason's right," the colonel agreed. "We need a plan."

"Well," said the Captain, "seeing how it will be mostly a land maneuver, I'm all for deferring the details to Mase. You're the best expert on how she thinks, anyhow."

"What do I know what she's got in that mixed-up head of hers?" Mason grumbled. "All I know is, if she thinks she can get away with something like this, she's got another thing coming."

By the time the *Dreadnaught* pulled up alongside the courtesy dock in Campbell River, nearly eight hours had gone by since Lou Edna had left the boat. So, it was a sombre group that headed off to scour near-by hotels and cafes where one might while away hours waiting for a flight back to the States. Not being able to catch an immediate flight out was really their only hope, considering the girl always had a stash of emergency funds for a quick escape.

It was a habit left over from living in so many dreadful places before Mason (who had done his banking where Lou worked), noticed she was all alone in the world, facing a terrible situation, and took her home to Millie. The two years she had been with "the family" were the longest she lived anywhere in all of her twenty-three years.

Considering how many boardwalks, malls, and shops were a short walk away from the waterfront, each of the five searchers chose a separate street, and agreed to "reconnoiter" after investigating four blocks. A thorough plan that would have cast a sufficiently wide net throughout the vicinity. Only they didn't need to carry it out. No sooner had they started up the docks to take up their positions, a frantic Lou Edna came flying down the ramp, hollering, "Pop—oh, Pop!" before she flung her arms around Mason's neck and cried, "You came back for me—you came back!"

"What did you expect, girlie? You left something important behind!"

"Cole said he'd be better off without me. And it's true!" She was dressed for obscurity (Stella knew a lot about runaways): jeans, navy-blue sweatshirt with tennis shoes and backpack. Little of her face was visible under a ball-cap and sunglasses. "But I just felt worse the farther I got away from him. Then I couldn't get back fast enough —you already left!"

"Had to leave early to catch the right tides," said Stuart.

"Cole didn't tell us you were gone until he got off watch at ten!" Millie sniffed as the girl flew into her arms next (like a chick returning to a mother hen). "What a scare you gave us, honey—what were you thinking?"

"I don't know. I was just trying to do right for my boy!"

"Two wrongs don't make a right," Stuart declared, in a tone loud enough to call all hands. "You jumped ship. No crew of mine ever pulled that on me before and I don't take kindly to it."

"Maybe we should talk about this when we get back aboard," said the colonel, noticing several onlookers nearby. "Especially since Gerald might slip into apoplexy the longer we're gone."

The engine roared to life as soon as they approached

—evidence that Cole was taking his part in the plan as serious as the rest of them had. Stuart left briefly to untie dock lines and set a course back toward the narrows, where they would pull over into a nearby cove and wait for the tide to turn. Again. Meanwhile, the rest of the group settled around the large wooden dining table in the galley to talk things over.

It had a brass lantern hanging above it that Stella had originally thought was simply for decoration. However, it was a fully operative kerosene lamp that gave off quite the cheery glow when it was lit. Something of a rarity on this trip because it stayed light until nearly bedtime around here. So, at the moment, there was plenty of light filtering in through the several large portholes in various places around the area. Gerald came in to join them, after Lou checked in on the baby, who was taking a late afternoon nap in the miniature swinging hammock his Uncle Gerry had set up for him in his own stateroom. In fact, they all had accommodations for the baby in their rooms since his mother was forever needing someone else to watch him.

"You should have at least talked it over with somebody," he was saying as the two of them returned to the galley. "Got a second opinion and all that. A decision made in haste almost never works out."

"I'll try to remember that next time I feel like jumping ship." Lou Edna sank down onto the edge of one of the upholstered benches and didn't take off her sun glasses, only pulled her ball cap down lower over her eyes. Another warning sign as far as Stella was concerned. People only wore sun glasses inside when they wanted to hide something. More lies, probably. She turned on one of the propane burners on the large iron cook-stove and set a huge stainless steel kettle on to boil. A cup of tea always made times like these go smoother, in her estimation.

"All right, let's have it." Mason removed his fisherman's cap and set it on the back of the seat. "And take those glasses off. I don't like talking to someone I can't see."

"I'd rather not," Lou Edna replied.

"Why in heaven's name?" Millie asked, and then gasped at her own unspoken answer. "Lou, you aren't—you didn't—"

"Girlie, you better not be," Mason interrupted. "We been through that, already, and once was enough."

The girl sighed and rested her head in her hands for a moment. "Sometimes, I just wish I was dead."

"Don't say that!" said Millie, who must have experienced similar thoughts during her own lowest moments and could identify. "Next thing you know, that's all you can think about."

"You've got a boy in the other room whose sun rises and sets on you," the colonel reminded her gently. It was the first time Stella could remember him saying anything encouraging to Lou Edna. "In his eyes, you're perfect."

"It's true," Stella agreed. "The greatest influence on any child is their own parents. It's a proven fact."

"He'll never forgive me," she mourned.

"What's to forgive?" Gerald argued. "He's so little he doesn't know the difference."

"Oh, somebody will tell him, they always do."

"Unless somebody else..." It was Cole's voice instead of Stuart's coming from the doorway as he came through. "Straitens up and makes some changes. So the kid at least has a mother he can look up to."

"Nobody can change what they don't feel, Cole."

"Who needs to feel it? Just find out what's normal and do it."

"You should talk. Right?"

"Well, he's right about that, anyway," the colonel pointed out. "Doing right is a precursor to feeling what's right. It's the way one learns to judge between right and wrong. Good and evil, you might say."

"Are you saying I'm evil, now, Mr. Colonel?"

"Don't get sassy, girlie," Mason warned. "And take off those sun glasses. You got people who care enough about you to try and help figure things out—show a little respect."

"I don't feel like it."

In answer, he reached across the table, lightly knocked the bill of her ball cap up and snatched them off. Only to reveal a glaring bruise that circled her left eye and the bridge of her nose. An audible gasp escaped Stella. Millie said, "Oh, no!" And Gerald leaped to his feet so fast he teetered then caught his balance before darting at Cole.

"Hey, wait a minute..." The younger man stood up to his full height and pointed a warning finger at the ridiculous figure coming at him in his half serape hanging over a green sweat suit "You just wait one minute!"

"Put 'em up!" Gerald danced back and forth on his feet in front of him and began to circle his fists. "You woman beater!"

"Don't make me pop you one, old man. You hear me?"

"Nobody's gonna pop anybody," said Mason. "Sit down, Gerry."

About three seconds before Gerald surprised everyone with a lightning-quick punch that knocked Cole DeForio in the nose so hard it started to gush blood, and sent him sprawling backward onto the floor.

5

Somebody hollered and the men got up to intervene. But it was unnecessary. Gerald staggered back at the realization of what he had done and sank down onto the nearest edge of the dining table so he wouldn't slip into a dead faint. Stella hurried to get a cold cloth to stop the bleeding, as everyone else hovered around Cole and tried to get him back on his feet, again. Which wasn't having much effect since he wasn't responding.

"Good grief—" Gerald pulled his watch-cap off and ran a hand through his thinning brown hair. "Isn't dead, is he? Didn't mean to do all that. Oh, I say!"

"He's out cold," Mason pronounced. "Where'd you learn to fight like that, Gerry?"

"Alarming number of people liked to beat up on me, when I was young, so I took boxing lessons. Don't know what came over me to hit him so hard. Must have done it in a blaze of anger."

"I'll say you did," said Lou Edna. "Serves him right!"

"He's coming to," the colonel observed just before the victim moaned and uttered a muffled curse.

Suddenly, there were two bells in rapid succession, then another two, and the young man struggled to get to his feet.

"You better stay put till the bleeding stops," Mason

suggested. "It's just Stuart wanting to drop the anchor outside those narrows and wait for the tide to change. And don't anybody go anywhere," he added as he started for the door that led out to the decks. "We're going to get to the bottom of all this, one way or the other. You hear me, Shortcake?"

"Pop, I came back—isn't that enough?"

"No."

"Well, I don't approve of any of it." Millie returned to the table and stirred three spoons of sugar into the tea she had poured from the things Stella set out earlier. "Resorting to physical violence is no way to solve problems."

"I agree," said Stella. "Cole, have you ever thought of taking a course in anger management?"

"Anger management—tell that to Lou. It was self-defense. She was hammering my gut like she was contending for some heavyweight championship."

"I don't have an ounce of fat on my body! Hit him, again, Gerry."

"E-gads—I'm still shaking from last time. I detest it when things get bloody, I really do."

"Lou Edna Wilson!" Millie set her mug down so hard tea sloshed out. "What on earth has gotten into you?"

"I'm regretting smuggling somebody aboard, that's what's got into me. Been all high and mighty ever since Cap promoted him. Like nobody else is good enough, anymore. I'd have taken the Senator with me if I didn't have to get another job and find a place to live, first. I wasn't really leaving him. I was going to send for him as soon as I got settled."

"And where were your going to send to—general

delivery, Alaska? We don't know exactly where the lodge is, we have to find it first. Then maybe it won't even be livable and we'd have to go somewhere else."

"Cap would have told me when he got back."

"Maybe he won't want to go all the way back. He's part of the family, now. But I have to tell you, Lou, it practically killed me you would leave without saying anything. After everything we've been through!"

"I'm not leaving you, Millie, I'm leaving him." She pointed to where Cole was still sitting on the floor with the wet cloth against his face. "What kind of mother would stay with somebody violent? But I knew you all needed him for crew so I didn't think I should say anything."

"Lou, if you tell one more lie, you'll be sorry," Cole mumbled from behind the cloth.

"Truth is the basis of all genuine relationships," the Colonel pointed out. A remark that caused Stella some discomfort because she still hadn't made time for that heart-to-heart she felt she owed him, yet, either. Even though she intended to.

"Keeping plans to yourself is not lying, Cole—I do not lie to this family!"

A statement that brought her young man up off the floor so fast, no one was ready for it. But instead of going after Lou Edna, he snatched the backpack she had set on the upholstered bench beside her, instead.

"Give it back to me!" she hollered. "Don't you dare!"

He dared. Even when she picked up Millie's tea and threw it at him, he only ducked and fended it off before unzipping and dumping the contents out on the table for all to see. Millie screamed. The colonel's eyes widened and his mouth dropped open, while Stella—who had stood up that very moment, in order to step between the two before they resorted to an out-and-out brawl—was just in time to catch Gerald before he fell off the table, onto the floor.

There was an assortment of credit cards belonging to various family members in the heap, the colonel's gold pocket-watch the military academy had given him when he retired, and several of Stella's autographed first editions from her book shelves. There was also a genuine shrunken head Gerald had paid a lot of money for on an archaeological dig in the South Pacific before his invalid days. But the things that had elicited a scream from Millie, and got her reaching for her heart pills, was the notorious *Villa Nofre* jewelry collection that belonged to the owner's last wife and had been missing for years.

"Where did you get those!" the mansion's former landlady could barely manage a frightened whisper.

"In a trunk up in the attic," Lou Edna admitted. "When I was looking for things to pawn that you wouldn't notice. Now, you'll probably never trust me again. None of you will!" At which point she buried her face in her arms on the table and gave way to more tears.

"E-gads—those things are worth a fortune—we could all go to jail for this. We're accomplices! What are we going to do, Mil? E.J.'s been a good sport but I doubt he'd let us off three times. First the household valuables, then the paintings, and now the missing jewels! He'd never believe us a third time!"

"Oh, I don't know what to do—Mason's going to hit the roof when he hears this! You couldn't have got away with pawning those, Lou. The family lawyers have had detectives and everyone else trying to find them for years.

The lady who owned them was a Russian refugee who came over here after World War II—some distant cousin to a Czar, or something."

"They're extremely well-documented," added Gerald, then grimaced at the very thought.

"We seem to be going from the frying pan into the fire every time we turn around, lately," said the colonel. "The amount of trouble this incident could have caused every one of us."

"Don't you have any feelings at all for us, Lou?" Millie implored. "We've shared everything we had with you, and you do something like this!"

"I didn't know they were that valuable—I didn't!"

"You definitely knew the value of everything else," said the colonel. "And a good idea of how to liquidate them, seeing how fast you were headed back home."

"What did you take us for?" Gerald pulled a handkerchief out of his pocket and dabbed at the beads of sweat gathering on his forehead. "A bunch of pushovers?"

"I'm afraid, that's exactly what she took us for," the colonel replied for her. "Except considering what terrible things might backfire in your own life as a result of this act, makes you something of a pushover, yourself, Lou Edna."

"Now, what am I going to do?" she wailed. "If my boy ends up in foster care, I'll kill myself!"

"That wouldn't help one bit," said Stella.

"I am a horrible person—just like Cole said! There's no hope for me!"

"Of course there's hope for you," said the colonel. "There's hope for everyone who truly wants it. You only have to ask."

"Nobody will ever forgive me for this—oh, I could just die!"

"There is one person who will," he replied. "And he already did the dying."

"What good would it be if I end up all alone? None of you will want me around anymore!"

"Young lady, you would never be alone in this world, again. That, I can promise you. With only a few words from you, right here and now, your entire life can be turned around. But it has to be genuine. You'd be talking to the one who knows every thought and intent of your heart, yet still loves you enough to give you a second chance. So... what do you say?"

6

"Stella," the colonel said later that evening, without looking up from his laptop. "You haven't read a word since you opened that book. Is there something bothering you? Something you'd like to talk about?"

"I just can't get over how Lou Edna responded to you. I even think that was a genuine prayer of forgiveness she prayed. Right in front of all of us."

"Well, it wasn't me she was responding to. I was just the messenger."

"But how did you know she was ready to pray? She jumped at your suggestion so fast, I think she was actually waiting to."

"I didn't know. But since she might never have a remorseful moment like that, again, I thought I better press the issue. Seems to have worked out."

"It certainly did. Why the change that came over her was practically instant. It was like you could almost see some great weight lifted off her. And it was so touching how Cole came over and hugged her so tenderly afterward. He must have a good heart, himself, to want so much for her to do things right. Maybe he was touched by the love of God at sometime in his life, too."

He smiled, then gave half a chuckle at the memory. "That's what really changes people, you know. The love of God. It's supernatural."

"Oh, it is!" she agreed. "In a good way."

"I'd say the love of God can't be anything but good."

"I was talking about the supernatural part. There are some supernatural things that aren't good at all. Wouldn't you agree?"

"Most definitely. But you wouldn't want anything to do with that sort of stuff, would you? Life is too short to fit everything in the world into it. And—as long as we get to choose—wouldn't you rather fill yours up with good things?"

"Of course I would. But sometimes we don't have any say in the matter."

"We always have some kind of choice, Stel. Sometimes it's only a very small one. But if you look close enough, you'll find it's a way out. Had that happen to me, personally, many times."

Stella thought how looking for a way out is what brought on the worst trouble in her life. But she certainly didn't want to get into that subject at the moment. The troubles at hand were more than enough to deal with. "I wish I could be that sure. I mean, it must be very comforting to have so much assurance."

"Well, I didn't get it all at once, you know. Just little by little, one choice at a time. Small adjustments, you might say. Life's full of choices—there are dozens every day. How's the saying go..." He cocked his head and thought for a moment. *"I have set before you life and death—oh, that you would choose life!* The more you practice choosing life, the better you get at it. Sort of a win-win situation."

"I hope Lou Edna discovers that. If she could only know that choosing to do wrong is what actually diminishes her opportunities. Not life being harder on her than anyone else. She's a smart girl, though. So, maybe it won't take too long for her to realize she can get better options to choose from each time she makes a good choice."

"Well spoken. And that's exactly what she would hear if she got some good counseling to overcome some of her past perceptions."

Stella thought how that was exactly where she had heard it but she didn't say anything about that, either.

"However—now that she's asked for it—she'll get plenty of supernatural help to make sure she succeeds," he went on, "as do we all. None of us are much of a match for the dark side of those spiritual realms. Some of us are just more susceptible to it than others. More easily taken in, you might say. Especially considering those dark forces have the ability to masquerade as creatures of light, for a time."

A thought that gave Stella something of a jolt—how in the world could a person tell the difference?

"The danger," the colonel went on, "is that their purpose is to trap you, not give you a way out of anything. They can only lead a person to death and destruction. No mortal is a match for that. Never has been. Which I suppose is why we get so tossed around between good and evil in the first place."

There was the opening. Stella realized, right then, that she needed to know how one went about getting that good kind of supernatural help, in order to escape the bad.

Because it suddenly became very clear that she had allowed frightening things to rule her life, too. So, she closed her book, took a deep breath, and jumped in.

"You know something, Oliver? I think I've been one of the deceived ones. Before I got my new life, I was convinced the only future I had was to end up in a good rest home instead of a bad one. I guess you could say I was a pushover for the darker side of supernatural, too."

"And look at you, now, Stel. Doing wonderful things a lot of younger people don't even get to do. You're on the adventure of a lifetime!"

"Makes me not want to ever look at the dark side of supernatural, again."

"And rightfully so. It's like opening up a can of worms. Nothing good can ever come of it. Just has some sort of curious appeal. Especially to people who are searching for something more than just everyday living. Which we all do at some point in our lives."

"That's sort of what I meant by not always having a choice with those types of encounters. Every once in a while something just... pops up in front of you and you bump into it. What I'm trying to say is... do you believe in ghosts, Oliver? Tortured souls that roam the earth for some horrid reason, or other?"

"I believe they aren't always tortured souls."

"What are they, then?"

He looked at her for a few moments, then closed his laptop and came over to join her on the couch. "Oh, I don't think it matters much, really. I only know there is no form of darkness that doesn't run for the shadows as soon as a light comes on. Which is why I make such a point of standing as close to the one who created light as I possibly can. That way, I'm not so apt to trip over things. None of us can see in the dark, anyway."

"I've certainly never thought of it like that before. But it does make more sense to look at it that way, now that you mention it. Especially since Gerald told me he's had more trouble since he started delving into those things than he ever had before that. Did you know he actually used to try to encounter ghosts? He studied old legends and went looking for them. Was even thinking of doing his master's on some ghost over in England. But he says he's never been the same since. Seems to be plagued with them everywhere he goes, now."

"My point exactly. If you ask me, it's half what's deteriorating his health."

"That's exactly what he said."

"Yes, and he's always after some new incantation to ward them off, too. You know he sleeps with tin foil over his head? That's why he wears a watch-cap to bed. To keep it in place."

"He's talked to you about it before?"

"Oh, we've had any number of talks about it. I advised it would be better to say a quick prayer and tell them to buzz off."

"You know, that's just what he did last night when I ran into him in the companionway. He called me a—a foul spirit—and told me to get away. Thought I was another one of his apparitions. That's what he calls them. Apparitions."

"I'd say that wasn't far wrong." Then he laughed trying to imagine the scene. "Just goes to show you never know when someone is really listening to you."

"Oliver?"

"Yes, my dear?"

"I've been seeing some sort of..." She smoothed a wrinkle out of the rose-colored throw she had over her lap. "Apparition, myself. A very distinct one, in fact."

"Well, the next time you do, say a prayer, and tell it to buzz off. Better yet—wake me up, Stel—and we'll face the thing down together!"

"Really?"

"Absolutely. '*If one can put a thousand to flight, two can put ten-thousand to flight*,' as the scripture says."

"It does?"

"Yes. You can always bank on the scriptures. They're truth in its purest form."

"Well, Oliver, I..." Stella looked at the man she had married barely a month ago, and suddenly felt as if she had found a rare treasure. And he wasn't even irritated with her! Now, the thought that he cared enough to walk with her even through the dark places gave her the most wonderful sense of well-being she had ever known. "Oliver Henry?" She slid closer and nestled into that comfortable, always ready, embrace that she loved so much. "I think you're the most amazing man I've ever known!"

"Believe me, I could say the same thing about you, dearest."

"Me? I don't think I've done much of anything amazing in my entire life."

"Oh, I don't know. I'll never forget the way you looked catching old Gerry before he fell on the floor. You're always the first to jump right in whenever something goes wrong. Remember when you wanted me to sign that petition to save good literature?"

"I remember I interrupted you when you were working on your hero book. But I didn't know that back then."

"Ah, I needed a good interruption right about then. I was getting too stuffy. You know, it takes an amazing woman to bring out the best in a man. That's what you've done for me." Then he gave her an affectionate squeeze. "What a match we are, Stella Madison Henry—I have a feeling we're going to make a great team!"

***

Every once in a while, someone comes along who can see the world through eyes of great understanding. If that person is also a good communicator they can help many people during their lives. But if that person also happens to be an artist, the world may keep their treasures throughout generations. Art—whether music, painting, literature, or drama—touches the heart faster than anything else. Especially if it's beautiful. And most especially if it mirrors some universal feeling that resides within the heart of all humanity.

Such was the case with Alfred Tennyson, who is one of the nine most quoted writers in the *Oxford Dictionary of Quotations*. A poet who ultimately became appointed by royal decree as the Poet Laureate of England and Ireland, he possessed the rare talent of not only being able express the deeper feelings of human experience but to express them in a way people did not want to ever forget.

As the son of a pastor, and raised in a moral home, he was blessed with a wonderful sensitivity and compassion for others. Being able to write about these feelings so beautifully became a mirror of common emotion that resonated throughout the world, even during his own lifetime. A good example is the quote at the beginning of this story which states in so few words, one of the deepest perplexities of life that we all eventually grapple with.

While it is human nature to seek after truth, it is also

one of our strongest impulses to try and separate ourselves from things that are false. So, anything that helps enlighten which-is-which for us, is a real gem. Such wisdom distilled down to its purest thoughts can be a great comfort during times of deepest stress, or sorrow.

In seeking out an appropriate quote for the subject of *The Pushover Plot*, I discovered that Alfred Tennyson was the author of many other wonderful quotes I had written into my notebooks over the years. So, the research for this little bit of truth I like to tack onto the end of each story, was more like a surprise visit from an old friend.

Maybe you will find that true, as well.

You can read more of Alfred Tennyson's work, for free, at:

http://www.gutenberg.org/files/8601/8601-h/8601-h.htm

To those who might suddenly find themselves wandering through wilderness places—may you be refreshed more than terrified.

LOST IN THE WILDERNESS

A Stella Madison Caper

"I have never been lost, but I will admit to being confused for several weeks."

Daniel Boone

Stella Madison opened the door to the after-deck and a blast of cold wind hit her face. Why did Millie want to meet out here? The galley of the *Dreadnaught* was so much more comfortable and cozy. Of course there was always someone else passing through it.

"I brought us some tea, Millie." She set the tray down on a small table between two deck lounges.

"Oh, thanks, Stel." Her former landlady set her knitting aside and tightened the black-and-white checkered scarf under her chin that she had wrapped around her auburn hair." Something hot would be good about now."

"It's awfully cold out here." Stella pulled her periwinkle blue knit cap down lower over her fluffy white hair that was just long enough to tuck under. and zipped her jacket all the way up.

"We're in Alaska, now. Mason says we have been ever since we crossed that Dixon Entrance, with all those fishing boats we had to dodge in and out of. Said if we didn't have to go all the way to Ketchikan to get back through customs again, we could be almost to the lodge by now. Mmm... Orange Spice. My favorite."

"Mine's the Moroccan Mint. Except Orange Spice just seemed warmer this morning." She sat down in the other lounge and unfolded a green wool blanket over her lap."Captain Stuart sure brought home a lot of souvenirs from his Navy days. Every lounge chair on this boat has one of these. Thank goodness."

"They're Army-issue. I think half the things aboard he got from one of those old Army surplus places back home."

"Well, looks aren't everything. They're nice and warm, anyway. Imagine being almost to the lodge, Millie. I can hardly wait to see it."

"Me, either. It will definitely be a load off my mind to get on solid ground, again."

"I thought you liked living on the boat."

"I do. It's got all kinds of ambiance. And that galley is heaven to cook in. It's the ocean I'm scared stiff of. Don't think I ever will get used to it." She set her cup down and picked up her knitting, again.

Stella was about to take another sip of her tea when she realized her friend's project was a sock with such an enormous tube it would go way past a person's knee, already. "Millie, who on earth is that for?"

"This? Oh, it isn't for anybody. I just knit to settle my nerves. The only thing I ever learned to do was socks. Way back when I was ten. Took me half the trip even to remember how to do it because it's been that long since I practiced." As if to prove the point, she began to unravel it, again.

Stella gasped at seeing the thing disappear into a heap

of wrinkly gray yarn right before her eyes. "But all that work—wouldn't you rather have something to show for it? Give them away for Christmas, maybe."

"They're not good enough for that. They always turn out crooked or something. But a person has to resort to some form of therapy when they're scared half out of their mind most of the time. Wouldn't you say?"

"I guess it depends on what you're scared of. The colonel says if it's something evil, you just tell it to buzz off, because you don't want anything to do with the dark side of supernatural. But if it's something legitimate like the ocean, I don't blame you. I was scared stiff myself during that storm we had. And I don't like it when it gets rough and choppy, either. But it must at least make you feel better that we're almost there."

"The truth is, Stel, I'm even more scared about getting there. Because of the bears. Mason says just make a lot of noise and stay in groups. On account of they don't want anything to do with us, either."

"Well, that sounds reasonable, don't you think?"

"Not as reasonable as having a loaded gun on my belt."

Stella wasn't sure if she would be more afraid of Millie walking around with a loaded gun than a bear but she didn't mention it.

"Bears you can shoot. But the ocean..." She got to the end of unraveling her sock and started casting on new stitches, again. "The ocean is so unpredictable and... big. I really don't know how Stuart even finds his way around in it. Especially without radar."

"We don't have radar?"

"Too expensive, and he never had the funds."

"For heaven sake, I didn't know that." She felt a twinge of apprehension at the very thought. "He's so confident about everything, I just assumed."

"Used to be confident. Which is really why I asked you to come out here, Stel." Millie stopped working, and looked her right in the eye. "Something is wrong with Stuart. He hasn't been himself the last couple of weeks."

"Well, he does have a lot more to worry about than the rest of us. The *Dreadful* being his boat, and all."

"It's the *Dreadnaught*, not the *Dreadful*. Sometimes I think you enjoy calling it that."

"I do. It's such a monstrosity of a thing. Although I have to admit it has its charm. I'll probably be won over by the time we finally get there." She took another sip of her tea and noticed Millie had dropped two stitches by the time she went back to her knitting. "But Captain Stuart has such peculiar ways, I don't see how you can tell if he's his normal self or not. He's one of the most abnormal people I've ever known."

"I can tell, all right. He only ate half his linguine and clams the other night and that's one of his favorite meals. He never used to miss when I made it back home."

"Maybe he's just not used to all our home-cooked meals. Didn't Mason say he lived mostly off boiled eggs, crackers, and sardines?"

"That and junk food. Which is why I decided to make hamburgers and fries for our celebration, tonight. That's his other favorite. The rest of of us won't mind as long as we barbecue and fill things out with your New England baked beans and Lou's fruit salad. If he doesn't eat any of that, we'll know something's definitely wrong. You think?"

"I'm thinking what would we do if anything happened to Captain Stuart. Maybe the rest of us should try to carry more of the load for a while. Could be he's coming down with something and just needs a rest."

"Could be. But I'm going to keep my eye on him during our Alaska celebration. Then slip him a good physic if I think he isn't quite right."

"Why, Millie—that's an awful thing to do to somebody. You should ask, first."

"He wouldn't take it at all, if I asked. Better just to slip it into his tea."

The celebration started somewhat early that night because the fog rolled in so thick they were forced to pull over into the nearest cove and anchor. Such places were numerous throughout the islands, and they were pure wilderness. Something that had little effect—other than offering spectacular scenery from every angle—to the small community of friends aboard the *Dreadnaught*.

Even fuel stations, which were few and far between the farther north they got, didn't really matter so much. Captain Stuart said they had enough to make the entire trip just on their original fill-up back in California. It was the one thing they wouldn't scrimp on and the main reason they opted to all sign on for extra "shipboard duties," rather than go to the added expense of hiring a professional crew. They also had the option of using the sails, which cut down considerably on fuel expenses all by itself.

Except there hadn't been much opportunity to use those sails. Going north, the wind was almost always "right on their nose," as the Captain called it, instead of on either side or behind them, where they could actually get some use out of it. Not to mention a sailboat of this size took practically a full gale to get it really moving (having been built more for ocean crossings). Not that they hadn't had to wait out a lot of gale-force weather pocketed away in some deserted place like this one. It's just that the combination of narrow channels, crazy strong currents and tides—as well as those gale-force winds—made for nightmare situations with such a novice crew. No matter how good everyone's intentions were.

Yes, Captain Stuart most probably had a lot on his mind.

Stella was thinking about all these things as she took her pot of New England baked beans out of the oven and set it at the back of the stove to keep warm. The men were out under a covered portion of the deck, overseeing the barbecue, and Millie was busy setting the huge table. Which looked especially lovely with the overhead kerosene lamp lit (dark clouds had moved in and it was already starting to rain) and a little blue pot of artificial white daisies the two of them had picked up in some dollar store at their last stop in Canada. Now, with nearly all of the long trip behind them, and their crossing back over into the U.S. earlier this afternoon, it was time to celebrate. They were finally in Alaska!

Even Millie seemed to have forgotten her dark worries of the morning, and cheerfully tucked one of those white daisies, that had fallen out of its setting, into her bountiful French twist as she hummed the same two lines of the old fifties classic, *Blueberry Hill*, over and over, again.

About then, Lou Edna, Cole, and the Senator came in from the forward companionway.

"Oh, my word!" Stella exclaimed as the little toddler with the big name reached out his arms to her. "If you aren't dressed like a regular little boy—rubber boots and everything!" She took him from Cole, who seemed especially cleaned up, himself, not missing the fact the two were both wearing jeans and the same blue sweatshirts.

"Cole says he won't know he's a boy unless we dress him like one." Lou Edna reached for another denim apron that hung just inside the walk-in pantry. "Besides that, he wore holes in the knees of all his bunny suits already, from crawling around so much."

"Wouldn't surprise me if he was walking before the month's out." Millie took the little boy from Stella when he reached out to her as soon as she got close enough. "Right, luvy? How about some fruit salad? It'll be awhile before those hamburgers are done, Lou."

"I'll just give him a cold hotdog."

"A baby can't grow strong living off potato chips and hotdogs. Wouldn't you say so, Stella?"

"Well, I wouldn't know so much about that," she replied. "But, as a teacher, I have heard it said that not having enough proteins and enzymes in the diet can lean toward tendencies of ADD. Which leads to behavior problems. Then—nine times out of ten—the authorities have to step in."

There was an audible gasp from Lou, as Stella had expected, since the young woman knew exactly what having to live under the supervision of authorities meant. Cole, who hadn't said a word during the entire exchange, reached for an apple from the fruit bowl on the counter, and gave her an appreciative wink before heading out the opposite door to join the men. By that time, Lou had her apron tied and was rummaging through the refrigerator for the fruit salad. Her blonde hair was gathered at the nape of her neck with a beige "scrunchie" that was a perfect match to the angora pull-over sweater which seemed somewhat the opposite of her usual t-shirt, jeans, and sweatshirt. She even had a set of lovely, teardrop pearl earrings on.

Then again, it was an evening of celebration and Stella thought it rather touching that she had even gone so far as to change the baby out of his usual pajama attire. Lou Edna had come a long way since her heartfelt decision to get on the right side of life (and the law) and change her ways. After a couple of weeks, the effects of the relief alone was softening her into a real beauty. The kind that came from inner peace instead of outward application. Come to think of it, considering how she used to get so overly made-up for her bank job every day, Stella couldn't remember seeing any of that once they all moved aboard the *Dreadnaught*.

Having made a mental note to keep an eye on whether or not Captain Stuart ate his dinner, was forgotten about halfway through the meal. It was during the discussion of what everyone's plans for the evening were. Usually, they lingered over coffee and dessert, swapping entertaining stories from varied backgrounds. However, if it was a weekend, or an occasion for celebration such as this one, they might go so far as to play a game of "Rummie," using shipboard tokens in lieu of cash, that could be traded for chores, favors, or some coveted food item a person might have a hankering for. Another favorite was to listen to some true account read from one of the volumes of hero stories that the colonel had chronicled over his years as a military historian.

Every bit of which went to the wayside when Lou Edna announced they had something entirely different in mind for this particular evening. If the Captain would agree.

"I got no complaints about most shipboard entertainments," he replied, adding more ketchup to a pile of French fries that was larger than his hamburger. "Long as it's legal."

"Lou and I were wondering if you'd marry us." Cole looked directly into the startled glance of the disheveled older man across the table. "You've done that before, haven't you?"

"I have. Got the service printed out in the back of my old seafarer's Bible. Along with funerals and other such things a captain might need to preside over."

"Well, then?"

" I think it's a fine idea," said the colonel. "Nothing seals a promise so much as an act that truly proves your commitment. It's the kind of trust between parties that one can't get any other way. More importantly, it's the right thing to do."

"I want to do everything right from now on." Lou Edna picked up a French fry the baby had deliberately thrown onto the floor and put it back on the tray of his high chair. "If doing things right could make you feel this good —how come nobody ever told me?"

"For one thing, you never let anyone tell you anything," said Mason. "As I recall."

"Neither do you, Pop," the girl countered. "Or you'd have married Millie a long time, ago."

"Lou Edna Wilson!" Millie gasped. "Mase isn't the marrying kind. He's always been up front about that."

"Something's either right, or it isn't," she muttered, bending down for yet another French fry that was gleefully pitched off the tray.

"Living by our convictions should always supersede trying to convince others to live by them, as well," the colonel pointed out. "Seems everyone's entitled to their own journey of discovery, no matter where it happens to land them. But as you found out so recently, Lou, some roads are more rocky than others."

"Wasn't my choice to be born there."

"No one else gets that choice, either. The only choice available is in getting off, or not. But it might help to know all roads lead to the same end. So, the fact that yours looked so much clearer, earlier on, will probably give you an advantage some of the rest of us—who chose later in life—never had."

A statement that launched an unguarded expression of satisfaction at Mason when Lou Edna looked back at him. And since everyone had rather naturally taken to considering the colonel the best source of spiritual judgment in their little group (simply because he had been working at it longer), the verdict, though unspoken, was pronounced. Something that caused the colonel to draw in his breath and stick out his lower lip in that expression of perplexity that was becoming so dear to Stella (such a tender-hearted man!). Because the last thing he would ever want to do was offend Mason, who was one of his original heroes.

So, there were a few awkward moments of silence when even the colonel was at a loss for words. Until

Mason suddenly banged his fist down on the table and pronounced, "Shortcake's right. Better make it a double, Stuart. So I can make an honest woman out of Mildred. Haven't been very happy with my own road, lately... and I could do with some of this peace and contentment I been seeing around here."

A sentiment that caused Millie to burst immediately into tears, and the baby right after.

At the precise moment Gerald pushed through the door from the outside deck with another plate of sizzling burgers and asked, "Anybody for seconds? Oh—I say! Now, what's wrong?"

And that was the reason—as Stella was to recall later —that nearly everyone's plate was left with something on it that evening. Especially since they decided to push things aside for later, and fully intended to come back to it all. Except that when Stuart returned from his cabin (presumably to get the old seafarer's Bible, to officiate services), a rather amazing transformation had taken place.

For the first time in the nearly two months they had been aboard the *Dreadnaught*, Captain Stuart appeared before them in a rather dashing black coat over a turtleneck sweater, with his gray hair that normally stuck out in all directions, slicked back and curling fashionably onto his collar. And considering Millie had scampered away to don a cheery floral-print dress (instead of jeans), and even Mason quickly shaved off his three-day bristle of whiskers and put on a clean denim shirt...

The unexpected occasion turned into a series of memorable tender moments that "the family" would never forget. It was their first day in Alaska, and in so many ways, their first day of a new way of life for all of them. So, the services—instigated by the youngest members (who would have thought?) --took place on the covered deck beneath the wheelhouse with all the rugged beauty of a mountain wilderness for a backdrop. There were even a few appreciative hugs and comments, afterward, for Lou Edna's determination to "do things right" that had propelled everyone to share in the whole wonderful experience.

Which could have been a perfect end to a perfect day.

Except just as they were all dispersing toward the various companionway doors that led out of the galley and toward their respective cabins, Lou Edna said, "Just in time, too. Because I'm going to have another baby."

Stella and the colonel stopped in their tracks, and Millie's, "Oh—Lou—Edna!" reverberated back toward them down the entire length of the hallway. That shocking news delivered so casually to those born with different values altogether, was the very reason the nightly ritual of listening to the weather channel was skipped, entirely. After all, they weren't on any specific schedule (other than their own), and tomorrow was another day.

There would be plenty enough time to get those necessary details in the morning.

3

The following morning they were socked in by a veritable "pea souper," as the Captain called it. One couldn't even see the trees on the edge of the nearby shore of the cove they were anchored in. Other than the first twinge of disappointment (they were so close to reaching their goal!), everyone soon settled into their various routines with the sort of resigned contentment that comes from having to wait on things one has no control over. There was always something to do and the same situation had happened to them on numerous occasions before.

So, the Captain and Cole took the opportunity to do some necessary maintenance on the engine, and Mason went back to carpenter-work on an overhead lighting project that connected two nightstands together, so Millie could get more reading done at night. She was working her way through Stella's library, even though she had never been much of a reader before.

Lou Edna, who rarely made an appearance before noon, had not so much as poked her head out of the spacious apartment she had made from the former crew's quarters in the lowest forward area of the ship. She had created a huge, rather ingenious play area for the baby that allowed for climbing over and between the various bunks via a cargo net tacked up and over them to prevent falls. With a collection of toys scattered within, and an occasional snack, he was happy to entertain himself until lunchtime.

Gerald was busy with his numerous studies of the many potted plants he had brought along. Who could tell which ones would thrive in such a climate? He had heard common vegetables could grow to enormous sizes in a place that had nearly twenty hours of sunlight per day this time of year. He was meticulously detailed in his charts and scientific journals. Such still being one of his few joys in life since he had retired from the Academic world, years ago.

As for Stella and the colonel, this was the best time of their day. The new book was coming along nicely and it seemed its author had never had such fun until he took up writing stories for boys. And with a wife to edit his rough drafts, who enjoyed bouncing new ideas around almost as much as he did, he was never happier. What's more, he was convinced—after all these years—he had truly discovered what he was not only best at, but made for. If one were to believe in that sort of thing. Which Stella did. Taking on his ambitions and philosophies had been as easy as taking his name. Mrs. Colonel Oliver P. Henry. She had never been happier in her life, either.

So the colonel was sitting at the old captain's desk, getting ready to enjoy an extra writing session since he would not have to take his stint at the wheel today. "Let's see..." He bent over the handwritten jottings in an open notebook where he had written his outline. "What are you boys up to next?" He ran a finger down to the appropriate place. "Ah, yes. The cave. You think you might find a good place to stash necessary supplies in case the whole world goes berserk. Well..." He opened his laptop and waited for it to take account of itself. "Think, again! Just wait till you see what's waiting for you in there!" Then he laughed with the pure pleasure of it and began.

Stella smiled from where she was sitting on the couch with her own laptop, going over his work from the day before. For a moment, she paused to think about several things that might be in such a cave... and then went back to the enjoyable task at hand. She had always loved reading stories for the middle-grades, and—after her years of teaching—knew quite a bit about boys, herself.

It was hardly an hour after that when they heard the thump of the engine starting up.

"What's all this?" remarked the colonel as he threw a look to the bank of French windows behind where Stella was sitting. "It's still socked in out there."

At which point there was a tremendous bang from somewhere in the depths of the vessel.

"Oliver—oh, what on earth?"

"Probably just Stuart readjusting his engine again, dearest. But maybe I better go make sure."

A few minutes later it seemed to be humming along just fine and a few minutes after that, it shut off, again. Stella breathed a sigh of relief that they wouldn't have to be venturing out in that pea souper after all, before she realized her own nerves were almost as stretched as Millie's. Captain Stuart's propensity to "nose out into the weather to see what it was going to do," was beginning to grate on her.

So, she felt even better when her husband reappeared a few minutes later to report, "Just changing out some hard-to-get-at hose, then using some kind of starter fluid that produces a big bang. Sort of a controlled burn, you might say. No need to worry."

"Well, thank heaven for that. It would be awful to have something go wrong when we only have a little farther to go."

"Indeed, it would."

However, the day only proceeded to get stranger from that point on. It was one of those days people find themselves considering whether they shouldn't have gone back to get up on the opposite side of the bed, in order to straighten things out. Because Stuart—always so careful to "do things by the book,"—suddenly decided to strike out across their last stretch of "big water," late in the afternoon. The Ketchikan Channel (not what it was formally called, but no one could pronounce the real name) being only about five hours away. Piece of cake after that because it was such a busy city, one merely had to follow a crowd of other boats back into the harbor. And considering it would still be daylight at nine pm, not much could go wrong.

The first thing that went wrong was a large rock at the entrance of their cove, which had been clearly visible when they came in, but was now covered over with a high tide. Even though the accidental bumping against it didn't cause any real damage, it served as a wake-up call to remind them of the necessity of having a spotter at the bow when entering or exiting such places. Rocks being the prevailing characteristic of the region. Why the depth sounder didn't give an alarm, no one thought to ask, because maneuvering in and out of tight places had always been the Captain's responsibility. In fact, if he hadn't been at the wheel that very moment, the danger might have caused serious damage.

Things simply went downhill from there. The afternoon wind kicked up stronger than expected, and Stuart's decision to skirt a little farther south of the fishing boats to avoid all those thousands of feet of net strung out across every available space on the U.S. side of Dixon Entrance, drove the *Dreadnaught* into six to eight foot waves, farther out. Why on earth had they even tried to attempt it at this hour?

That's what Stella was thinking when the ship's bell summoned "all hands on deck" to hoist sails.

Heading directly north was no longer an option. Now, they must use the wind to stabilize the ship so they could plow through the waves instead of rolling into the steep troughs each time they were hit form the side. They were sailing directly out into rough weather, and another storm at sea. However, the crew was more seasoned this time, and understood their jobs much better than those early days. Which was the only reason they managed to "beat into it" for nearly three full hours before finally raising a distant shore where they could find another safe cove or inlet, to slip into. Who cared how far off course they were? Everyone was exhausted.

Something that only added to the strain on nerves when the place began to disappear on and off, behind patches of clinging fog the wind was still trying to blow off the rugged land. So, they took a compass bearing on a point that looked promising and strained all eyes for any sign of unexpected rocks that might be strewn out in front of it. At least the seas began to settle down the closer they got to land. But so did the wind. Down with the sails, again, and the last hour was a nightmare, before Lou Edna (who had the best eyes aboard) called out a possible opening. A tight squeeze, but they would have to take it.

Because night was already coming on.

So, they began to snake their way up a long, narrow inlet that seemed to have no sign of widening out, at all. Cole stood at the very tip of the bowsprit, giving hand-signals up to the wheelhouse as they inched their way around the rocky shores at a snail's pace.

"Over there!" Lou called down from her perch on the mainmast yardarm. "Big enough to turn around in!"

"Port, or starboard?" insisted Cole.

"On the right—the right—I mean, starboard!"

He gave the signal but there was no response from the wheelhouse. "Get down here and take over, Lou. Colonel and Mase—get ready to let go the anchor. Millie, keep an eye out for rocks off the port side and holler out soon as you see any. Mrs. H, you come with me."

Which is how it came to be that Stella was the only witness to exactly what happened, next.

She followed Cole up the short steep ladder to the topmost deck of the *Dreadnaught* (lagging considerably behind the quick agility of their dark-haired First Mate), and was shocked to arrive in time to see him thrust the older man aside and take over the wheel so forcibly that their captain fell into a crumpled heap onto the floor. She had read enough sea stories to know such an act was nothing less than mutiny, but didn't know exactly what she should do about it. Other than rushing to the side of

Captain Stuart, only to discover that he was completely unconscious.

At which point there was an ear-splitting scream of "Rocks! Rocks!" from Millie, before Cole immediately spun the wheel hard over and...ran right over them.

Stella was picking herself up off the floor before she even realized she had toppled over. There was screaming and hollering (Millie, mostly) and a tumult of running feet clamoring over the decks below. Were they sinking? By the time she pulled herself up enough to look over at Cole, the young man was standing with his back to her, his head sagging down to his chest, and still hanging onto the wheel. But only for a few moments before he gave a great sigh and shut off the engine.

"Is he alive?" he finally asked without turning to see for himself.

"I..." She was still on her knees, and only had to lean over to look at Stuart. He seemed to be sleeping. She gave his shoulder a gentle shake but there was no response. "I think so. Yes, he's breathing, anyway. Cole—what on earth possessed you to push him so—"

"Something happened. He was froze to the wheel."

"Dear Lord..." She patted the Captain's face, trying once more to wake him. "Maybe we better not move him right away. At least not for a while." She took off her jacket and slipped it under his head, then reached for the army blanket on the nearest chair, to unfold over him.

"I better go check how much damage there is."

He slipped out the door, and was barely gone when Gerald clamored in from the companionway that led from the galley beneath them. He was wearing a bright orange life-jacket, and carrying the Senator over his shoulder, buckled into a miniature of the same. "Millie's gone over the side," he panted. "Saw the whole thing from the galley port when we were getting into our life-jackets. Just—pffft!—popped over like a cork out of a bottle because she was leaning out over the rail too far."

"For heaven sake! Is she—"

"Pfft! Just like that! Had her lifeline on, though, so they hauled her right up. Didn't even get wet, that's how high up we are. What happened to Stuart?"

"We're not sure. Cole said he was frozen. Just hanging onto the wheel." She moved over to where she could look down on the forward deck. It was tilted back at a slight angle and looked eerily deserted. Where was everybody? Were they sinking? What if they had to abandon ship out in this—oh, dear God!

All at once, a single shaft of light broke through the dark clouds as the sun was going down between two magnificent mountain peaks. It gave the illusion of resting right on top of the *Dreadnaught*. In that light it looked as if their ship had nosed close up into a narrow meadow nestled between those two pine-covered mountains. And—what was that? A waterfall tumbling down from somewhere high up, over a wall of rock, not too far away.

Stella felt a sudden sense of profound peace, along with the fleeting thought they had landed in the prettiest place they had come to, yet. Then it occurred to her how often their situation could change (so instantly!) after she prayed for God to save them out of some circumstance that seemed to be pressing her beyond her own personal limits. Almost before she even knew what to pray for. As if simply calling out to God during those times was enough for Him to intervene.

Gerald handed her the baby, and then bent down to have a better look at the Captain. "Seems like he's...had some kind of stroke."

"Oh, I hope not!" She settled the toddler onto her hip. "It could be hours before we can get any kind of help way out here."

"More than that I'm afraid. Something busted up forward. Right under the boy's play area. I daresay there was water trickling in when we left."

Stella felt her stomach lurch as if she had just gone down fast in an elevator. "Are we—sinking?"

"Nobody's sinking," replied Mason, who came in at that very moment to switch on the VHF radio. "Just knocked a board loose because somebody didn't know right from left. What are you trying to do, Gerry—scare the women?"

"Best to plan for the worst, I always say."

"Well don't. Cole's got the pumps going, already, and the Colonel's setting up the tools. We'll have it fixed even before help can get here for Stuart. How's he doing? Cole said he passed out for a while."

"A while—he hasn't come out of it, yet." Stella informed him. "Gerry thinks it might be a stroke."

Mason's face registered a combination of remorse and despair as he looked over at his long-time friend, lying so still beneath the green blanket. But only for a moment. After that, he returned his attentions to the radio with renewed vigor. "What's wrong with this thing?" He banged on it and twisted a few more dials. "Probably been busted for years, like everything else around here!"

Gerald's face went pale beneath his black Navy watch-cap. "If we can't call for an emergency helicopter..." His brown mustache quivered. "How the—devil—do we abandon ship?"

"We can't abandon ship," Mason sluffed out of his army-green rain-jacket, now that he was inside and dropped it on a chair. "We've got everything we own on here."

At which point Stella felt her knees go weak and murmured something about getting a bottle for the baby, so she could at least find some place to pull herself together. Anything to keep from being overwhelmed at the thought of being shipwrecked. Shipwrecked! Right out in the middle of... why, she hadn't the faintest idea where they were in the middle of. And without Stuart to figure it out...

It was a quiet, sombre crew that sat around the table in the galley, two hours later.

The situation was more grim than they first realized. They had set up a cot in one corner so they could bring the Captain in and keep a close eye on him. He still couldn't be wakened. In the meantime, they discovered that not only did the radio in the wheelhouse not work, neither did the weather radio in the galley. Considering they weren't getting much more than static across all channels, they wondered if they might be too closed-in by surrounding trees and mountains to get any reception. They tried to send out a message anyway, but there was no response.

After two months aboard the *Dreadnaught*, they knew enough to get the ship into some safe harbor, even if they didn't know exactly where they were. Or, at least close enough to some fishing boat to ask for help. Except they were stuck fast on top of the rocks they had run over. A fact that turned out to be their salvation, considering the damage had been more extensive than they first realized. While water was only trickling into Lou's apartment, it was fairly pouring into the lower hold, where most of their supplies were. The jolt had opened up a larger crack between the boards, down there.

It might have spelled disaster if the water hadn't stopped rising when it reached a level of two feet at the lowest end of the vessel. This because they had run high enough up on the rocks to be about three-quarters out of the water everywhere else. Which should have made them feel safer. Except the knowledge that the water fell off to depths of nearly a hundred feet on either side, made them realize where they might have been—this very minute—if they hadn't run so hard aground.

Something they had to credit to Cole for thinking so fast. But while they were not sunk, they were definitely not going anywhere. At least not anytime soon. Maybe even never, if the tide didn't rise sufficiently to float them back off the rocks, again. And even though there was always the hope that someone else might wander into this same place and find them, who knew how long that would take? The only thing they did know was they were in some wild corner of the Pacific Ocean where most of the of the smaller islands they had been traveling through were uninhabited.

And there were hundreds of them.

Of course, there was always the possibility they had landed on the shores of one of the larger ones, but—after so many weeks of passing through mile after mile of wilderness places—the chance of that would be be an out-and-out miracle. That being the case, they decided they might as well go to bed and tackle the problem, again, in the morning. That is, everyone except Gerald, who volunteered to sleep on the long upholstered bench at the back of the table, there in the galley, in case Stuart woke up and didn't know where he was or what had happened.

By that time, it was nearly midnight.

As exhausted as Stella was, she remembered thinking —just before she drifted off to sleep—that she had never faced any disaster with so much calm and assurance as she felt just then. Maybe it was because she never had so many people to face one with before. Then, again, it could be that having such a strong, wonderful husband (who always made the best of things) helped her feel like she could survive anything, too. Whatever it was, she knew— someplace deep in her heart—that everything would work out right. Somehow. Simply because God promised it would. It was a feeling she had never experienced, and the only reason she was able to fall into such a deep, restful sleep under such terrible circumstances. Which was a good thing.

Because it only lasted about an hour.

First, there was a scream (but not Millie's). Then a terrible lot of banging and commotion that seemed to be coming right down the companionway toward their door. The colonel jumped up and took off toward it in his navy pajamas (with gray piping), but Stella grabbed her white terry robe (with the Chinese collar) to put on over her rose-colored silks before following after.

She got there just in time to see Gerald tumble into the room with such a horrified expression, her first thought was that Captain Stuart had passed on and already begun to haunt them for wrecking his boat. A thought she stoutly rejected, considering her new-found faith that God could —and would—save her from anything so frightening. If she would only ask. Except she didn't get a moment to. Not ten seconds later, a staggering form emerged out of the dark passageway and grabbed Gerald from behind, eliciting such agonizing shrieks and moans that Stella screamed (she couldn't help it), and darted behind the huge protective bulk of her husband as he grappled to separate the two.

"Here, now—what's this—what's this?" He finally

managed to get in between them. "Stuart—Stuart! Everything is fine—I assure you, sir! Come over to the couch and I'll explain." Words that had a settling effect on the haggard form. Almost like a balloon slowly losing its air.

The colonel helped him over to the settee and it was then Stella noticed his right arm was dangling lifeless at his side and he was dragging a leg along like it was weighed down by some invisible ball and chain. She felt a catch in her throat that Gerald hadn't been far wrong when he guessed the man had been stricken by some sort of stroke.

"What a—ghastly experience!" Gerald whispered aside to her, and rubbed a hand over his throat at the same time. "He tried to choke me! I heard him shuffling around and—before I could even get out of my sleeping bag—he tried to choke me!"

There was another garbled moan directed at the colonel this time and it was clear he was trying to speak but couldn't manage a comprehensible word. The right side of his face seemed to have drooped and become immobile, adding a rather grotesque expression to his already rugged features. Especially with those bushy black eyebrows that nearly made a solid line across his forehead. Her husband drew in a breath and smacked his knees (she knew that decisive gesture well) before he said, "Well, sir, it seems you've had an episode of sorts."

Stuart gave out with another moan, mournful this time, and a look of abject misery crossed over his face.

"Always the possibility that symptoms are temporary however," the colonel went on. "You've been unconscious for hours. We weren't even sure you'd come back to us. But you did. A man of your strength and spirit, why, I believe—with the proper rest and care—you most certainly will recover!"

It was a statement that should have had a more calming effect on the man (it certainly did on Stella and she agreed whole-heartedly). But instead, he began to get agitated, again, banged his good arm against his leg, and tried once more to speak. At which point Millie burst in (wearing only a nightgown), with Mason not far behind, clad in sweats and a sleeveless undershirt.

"Stuart—oh, you're alive—thank God!" she cried. "We're in terrible trouble!"

A statement that caused the poor Captain to lapse into more audible frustrations.

"Mildred, for crying out loud!" said Mason. "You want to give the man a heart attack on top of it? Listen here, Stu—"

It was at that time Cole strode through the door, shirtless and barefoot, with only a pair of hastily donned jeans on. Lou Edna was close behind, also barefoot, in a long purple t-shirt that only covered the necessities, and her hair hanging loose over her shoulders. The rest of them naturally parted to let him through (he was the only one with any rank or knowledge of the sea left among them)—their new leader by unspoken consensus, even though he was young.

He leaned over to put firm hands on each of Stuart's shoulders and their eyes locked. "I had to put her on the rocks, Cap. It was too late to go around. But she can't sink. We got a hundred and thirty feet of water on one side, and eighty on the other. Little less than fifty to the shore. We're good."

A visible wave of relief came over him.

"Too closed-in for the radio, though," he went on. "Tomorrow, I'll run the skiff out into the open and try and flag down some help. We're good." He continued to hold on for a minute as if the man might topple over if he let go, then repeated, "We're good," before he stood up straight, again.

All at once, the old captain seemed unbearably weary and it looked as if he might fall asleep, again, any minute.

"Might as well stay in my cabin," said Mason. "It's closer to everybody, and you won't have to go down any stairs. I'll bunk in with Millie. Been spending most of my time there, anyway."

So, the men helped him up and settled him there, while the women murmured their second good-nights of the long day and drifted back to their beds.

6

The following morning brought rain and wind, along
with a constant current of ripples in from the choppy strait
outside the inlet. The barometer was falling, signifying
another weather front coming in. While it made little
effect on their solidly grounded vessel, there would be no
venturing out into storm-tossed seas in the little skiff to try
and seek help from other passing boats. Few people
would be fishing out there today, wherever they were.

But even though the day was gray and raining
torrents, it was plain to see they had landed in the most
beautiful, picture-postcard of a place. And although it
was only August, the little meadow that stretched away
into the mountains was already tinged with the red and
gold hues of fall. That particular morning, there was a
mother deer with two babies grazing not far away—a
sight that cheered the family up considerably in spite of
their dire circumstances. This was Alaska!

At any rate, it seemed to stir everyone out of the shock
of the night before and it suddenly seemed clear what they
should each be doing. The men were going to get
seriously busy on the repairs that had only been
temporarily patched and the women, having spied a huge

stand of bushes fairly sagging with huckleberries close by, were going to take the little skiff into shore for a land expedition. They thought.

Not long after they announced those plans Mason established a new rule that none of them were to leave the ship without at least one of the men along. Something they all quite naturally accepted since he was an expert on survival. Not only had he lived on his own for weeks, back in the jungles of Viet Nam, but had managed to save others along with himself while he was doing it.

So it was, that Lou Edna bundled the Senator into her backpack-carrier, appropriately dressed in a tiny yellow rain-hat and slicker that made Stella think of the famous *Paddington Bear*, of children's literature. Was there anything more adorable? The rest of them were bundled into rain-gear as well, armed with a sufficient amount of gallon-sized plastic bags stuffed into their pockets to bring home a treasure-load of berries.

Cole came along to handle the skiff and provide the necessary male supervision their new rule required, although he made it clear—right up front—he had no desire to pick any berries. Millie made a bet with him then and there, he would be venturing into those bushes all on his own as soon as he got a taste of her "Huckleberry Betty." The windfall wouldn't be around much longer but if they took advantage of it, there would be enough berries to provide jam and desserts throughout the whole winter. Wait and see.

No one knew how to store up food, like Millie.

It took longer to get everyone over the side and situated in the skiff than to cross the fifty feet of deep water to the shore. It wasn't until then that Stella realized she hadn't set foot on land since that last Canadian town where they had found the dollar store. Almost three weeks, ago. The first thing that struck her was the delicious smell of the air. It was a combination of pine trees, rich earth, and the sea.

Cole set out for the top of a nearby hill to have a look at the waterfall but promised to not be more than a shout away in case they needed him. Lou Edna took the baby carrier off her shoulders and set it down in such a way that provided a perfect perch for the Senator to enjoy a morning snack of graham crackers and watch the festivities. It was at that point Millie briefly unfastened her raincoat to get at all her plastic bags, when Stella noticed she had a huge leather holster with a pearl-handled gun sticking out, strapped to her waist, underneath.

"It's a specially-made, three-fifty-seven magnum," she replied to Stella's sudden gasp. "My first husband bought it for me back in our prepper days."

"Good grief, Millie—can you actually shoot it?"

"Of course I can shoot it. Took lessons, and everything. I'm a pretty good shot, too, even if I say so, myself. Wouldn't want to run into any bears without it."

The thought suddenly occurred to Stella that she better inform Cole about this before he got too far away. She would tell him to be sure and make plenty of noise coming and going, so he wouldn't get mistaken for a bear. Something that would also give any nearby bears a warning to keep their distance, as well. She did not want her friend take a pot-shot at one (that didn't hit home) and only make it mad. Stella had read enough bear stories to know such things happened more often than not when all parties had their attentions distracted by berries.

But it wasn't so easy to catch up with Cole and she finally had to call out to him. He turned around and waited for her. It wasn't until they were close enough that she noticed how upset he looked. Maybe he and Lou Edna had argued, again.

"Sorry to break in on your quiet time," she spoke first. "But I thought I should warn you to make plenty of noise on your way back because Millie's packing a gun."

He murmured something Stella didn't quite catch under his breath and shook his head. "If there's one thing I got to say about this group, it's nobody's boring." He sat down on a large, nearby rock and looked out at the view... a gray desolate expanse of rock-strewn inlet (so many of them were visible now that it was low tide), and the *Dreadnaught* perched on the tallest cluster, like some giant bird with a broken wing. "Did anyone tell her you can't drop a bear with some lady's pea-shooter?"

"Oh, it isn't a pea-shooter. It's a... what was it, now... oh, yes. A three-fifty-seven magnet."

He laughed, and shook his head, again.

"Anyway, that's what I thought she said." Stella sat down next to him. "Of course, I've read a lot of Louis Lamore westerns and know most handguns aren't accurate at long distances. Either way, it's an accident waiting to happen, so maybe you should holler out before you come down. So you don't startle her."

"Thanks. I'll do that."

He was quiet for so long that she got to her feet, again. "Mrs. H?"

"Yes?"

"How did a person like you end up getting mixed up

in all this?"

"Well, I guess you could say I had the fine good fortune to get a second chance at life. So, even with these, umm... unusual circumstances, I'm still having a marvelous time."

"You think you can forgive me for being so rough with Cap?"

"Well, of course I forgive you. I admit I was shocked to see you push him like that. But..."

"I had to get him off the wheel. He was stuck to it like rigamortis set in and I knew we were gonna hit."

"Oh, I understand all that, now. The colonel says we would have sunk if you hadn't run us up onto the rocks so hard. On account of it being so deep around here."

"We'd have lost everything if we did. Gerald and Buddy... they never would have made it up from below fast enough. Even if they had, that water's way too cold for either of them."

Stella suddenly realized how sensitive he was. Funny how tender hearts were often housed in the toughest of bodies. And she was touched that he had even taken her suggestion and come up with a name of his own to call the Senator, the way all the rest of them had. He seemed to have taken on the responsibility of actually being a father to the little boy. As far as Lou Edna would allow anyway. "It was exactly the right thing to do, Cole. I find it amazing you could even think that fast."

"Sorry I had to be so hard on Cap, though. Didn't mean to cause him any brain damage." He shook his head and looked out at the view, again. "I love that old man!"

"You did not cause brain damage," she replied firmly. "His brain was starting to misfire before we even got here.

Millie noticed it over a week, ago. She mentioned it to me."

"Well, getting shoved on his ear didn't help it any. Thing is, I lost my folks early. Been hanging around waterfronts—working my tail off—since I was fourteen. He's the only one ever gave me any kind of break. The only one. I just..." He took a deep breath and leaned his forearms across his knees. "I just wish I could have done better for him."

Stella sat down next to him and rubbed a comforting hand across his broad shoulder. "I think he knows that. You're the one he responds most to. The one who doesn't patronize, and tells him the absolute truth. If you ask me, I'd say he feels the same way about you."

"Well, you can bet I'm going to take care of him for the rest of his life. Because what he did for me? I don't take that light. Lou and I talked about it, and we both feel the same—"

There was a loud, resounding blast, a startled yelp from Lou Edna, and the baby started to cry.

"Holy—crud!" He leaped to his feet. "She better either missed it—or killed it!"

Stella didn't even try to keep up with him as he took off down the hill. But if it had been anything serious there would have been a lot more hollering and screaming by now. Instead, Mason's voice boomed over the water from the after-deck where he was working, "Mildred—what did I tell you about that thing!"

"I thought I saw something in that tall grass up there, Mase! False alarm."

Stella breathed a sigh of relief as she picked her way down the incline at her own careful pace. It was a lot easier going up than down. All at once, she saw someone stick their head up out of the grassy meadow a short distance away and their eyes met with the same identical expression. Who on earth? Before she realized it was the head and shoulders of a bear. Her first thought was that it had such intelligent eyes. Almost like a person's. What a shame it would be to kill such a creature!

"Go! Go that way!" she whispered, pointing in the opposite direction before continuing on her own way down the hill. Oddly enough, the bear—almost as if it understood—moved off toward the trees just as quickly. It wasn't until later that she realized she hadn't felt even a flutter of fear.

Another miracle!

The weather front hung in place, pouring a deluge of rain down on top of the castaways for an entire week. During that time they discovered more accurately how long it would take to get the boat operational again, and then off the rocks. If no help came it could take weeks. And though they had plenty of resources aboard for repairs—knowing the lodge would most likely be in terrible shape from having been vacant for so many years—they didn't know exactly what kind of place that was, or if it even still existed. For all they knew it could be nothing more than a tumble-down shack sitting in the middle of some swamp.

So, they had some decisions to make.

The majority of which really belonged to Stuart. They had dragged the man from one end of the ship to the other, lowering him over the side in a "bo'sun's chair" to see the damage, or even bundled into his rain gear to get a look at the work area they had set up on shore.

A make-shift bridge had been constructed early on by felling two trees and then hammering short pieces of wood across the top for a boardwalk. Something that saved a considerable amount of time and effort in hauling things back and forth between the boat and the shore.

On the occasions Stuart needed to come across, Cole simply hoisted him onto his back in a "Fireman's Carry" and hustled him over the bridge to his supervisor chair. It was one of the deck chairs tucked under a tarp-covered area where Mason had set up the portable sawmill he brought along for making lumber.

They had been making lumber ever since they got there.

It soon became evident that the Captain's mind was as sharp as ever. He had simply lost the ability to speak or move around easily. A situation that still occasionally threw him into a rage of frustration. One that almost always simmered down somewhat with a reassuring clap on the shoulder from the colonel, and the remark, "It's only temporary, sir—only temporary!"

However, it was Stella, and her many years of having to deal with mentally deranged people, who had come up with the ingenious system of communication that worked best for him. She did it by keeping several washable markers at the table. The ones Millie used for the little white-board tacked up in the pantry to keep track of stores. A different color for each member of the family.

The large wooden dining table was lacquered so smooth that it made the perfect surface for him to write or draw on, then erase with a damp cloth. And even though it often turned into a game of Charades, trying to figure out what he meant (his right hand was not usable, so he had to struggle with his left), it was at least immediately apparent by which color he picked up, who that particular message was for. That and a few gestures, such as a nod or shake of the head for yes, or no. Thus, he was reinstated as the top-ranking voting member of the party.

So it was, that he sat at the head of the table (it was their first Sunday afternoon since the disaster), armed with his markers and a cup of tea poured into one of the Senator's "sippy cups" (most liquid he drank tended to leak out the slack side of his mouth, otherwise) and—on this occasion—a notebook and pencil. Signifying he was going to attempt to communicate something important.

The meeting was called to order.

"What a blessing we've brought our own little world into the wilderness with us," observed the colonel, as he finished off the last bit of Millie's Huckleberry Betty. "To be in a situation like this and still have the sort of comforts we enjoy aboard the *Dreadnaught*. Light, warmth, superb food, and the coziest of homes...mmm! Must be a sermon in that, somewhere."

"Speaking of such," said Mason, helping himself to another cup of coffee, "you being the most educated on that subject, I was thinking how it would do us all good, under the circumstances, to share some of what you been talking to Shortcake about. I'm ashamed every time I have to agree she's right, lately."

"It's just I have a lot of questions, Pop. I've been doing things wrong my whole life. And Mr. Colonel says—"

The baby, who was standing on the upholstered bench between her and Cole, suddenly stopped playing with the Jello boxes Millie had given him, and leaned against her to jabber into her ear.

"The colonel says," she repeated as she automatically stacked the boxes into a tower for him, again, "the only way you can change your wrong thinking is by learning what's right. Then practicing that until God miraculously changes your mind."

"I believe that's a Lou Edna paraphrase for Romans 12:2," the colonel interjected. "Where it states we can actually be transformed by the renewing of our minds. Once again, it's a decision we all individually have to make."

"All I know is it took a miracle to change me." The toddler knocked his boxes down again, and she reached under the table to pick two off the floor.

"Like I always said," replied Mason. "Didn't think you'd ever change, since I thought it couldn't be done. Anyway, a little Bible reading on Sundays wouldn't hurt any of us. Right, Stuart?"

The Captain shrugged, but only one shoulder went up.

"He doesn't mind," interpreted Gerald.

"Then it would be an honor," the colonel agreed.

"All right, then." Mason took a folded piece of paper out of the pocket of his red and black flannel shirt. "Now for the items up for a vote."

Millie stopped wiping off the stove and came to sit down next to him. Stella linked her arm through the colonel's and sighed with contentment as she looked at the whole family seated around the table.

"First up, we have to decide whether we should just stay right here for the winter. Point being we don't know when, or if, we're going to get help. If so, there's things we can do before the cold weather comes to make it more comfortable around here. Such as blocking the back end of the boat up, so we can get rid of this cock-eyed slant we been walking around on. Thing is, it would take some time away from repairs to do it."

"If we do get help," said Gerald, "I volunteer to go with Stuart, so he can get some medical. Or, at least some therapy on..." His hand involuntarily felt for his throat. "How to deal with all this."

The Captain tossed the green marker at him with his left hand and bounced it off his head.

"Oh, I say!" Gerald replaced it in the pile.

"We'll cross that bridge when we come to it," said Mason. "Any opinions up for discussion?"

"Well," Millie spoke first. "Considering our original plan—before E.J. let us off—was to disappear somewhere in Alaska, it's not like we didn't come prepared to do something like this. The only hard thing is being totally cut off from the rest of the world. Which is something we can't do anything about right now, anyway. So... I vote, yes."

"Me, too," agreed Stella. "We came to experience Alaska, and this is about Alaska as it can get."

"It would definitely give me enough time to finish my novel," the colonel put it. "Might be rather freeing, not writing to a deadline for once. I couldn't accept a contract on speculation, now, even if I wanted to. No Internet, no telephone, no post office. I vote, yes, as well."

"So, it's down to the DeForio family, then," said Mason.

"This is the best I ever had it," Cole admitted.

"I don't care what we do," Lou Edna added. "If I didn't have this family, I'd have killed myself by now."

"For heaven sake, Lou," Millie admonished. "Don't give me such a start this early in the discussion."

"Well, it's true."

"Stuart?" Mason looked over in time to see another

one-shouldered shrug.

"He doesn't mind," said Gerald.

"Passed. Point number two. It occurred to me we should establish a signal fire. Could be we got ourselves farther off than we thought and ended up buried into some national wilderness area no one ever goes to much."

Stuart gave out with a bellow and reached for Mason's red marker. But instead of writing anything, he merely jabbed at the air over the top of the carpenter's head with it.

"Oh, right." Mason raised up in his seat enough to get the last chart they had been navigating by, that was rolled up and stashed behind the back of the bench. "Stu thinks we're somewhere around..." He slid the rubber band off and unrolled it for everyone to see. "Here."

He pointed to a cluster of little islands off the southwest tip of the Alexander Archipelago, that lay between the Pacific Ocean, the West Dixon Entrance, and the South Prince of Wales Wilderness. Ketchikan was at least sixty miles to the northeast, and the nearest other town was... they all stared silently at the vast amount of space... the closest seemed to be a logging camp, situated on the largest island. But that was even farther away than Ketchikan.

"That being the case," Mason went on, "a continuously burning fire might be the only thing that would catch anyone's attention this far out. At least by some passing plane that could report it to the Forest Service, maybe. So..." He looked up at the group, again. "We got to set fire watches throughout the day to man it. Two at a time is best, in case of..." He rubbed a hand over his three-day growth of salt-and-pepper whiskers.

"Something happens."

"Lou and I will do the early watch," said Cole. That way I can take the skiff out the inlet before the tide changes and look for any boats out there."

"I hate early mornings," complained Lou.

"You just haven't seen enough of them," Cole replied.

"OK. Cole and Lou on the first one, then." Mason wrote it down on the back of his list. "Who's next?"

After they had each chosen their times for the fire watch, the third order of the day was the announcement of their need to conserve diesel.

"But, why?" Millie asked. "We're not even going anywhere."

"Because the generator that makes your electricity runs off diesel," he answered. "And—in case you haven't noticed—there wasn't a lick of sun, this week to use Stuart's solar-powered system. Not to mention we're in the middle of a rainforest, here. So, it could be like this most of the time from now on."

"Oh."

"I imagine we're running close to empty, anyway," the colonel pointed out, "since we haven't added any since we left California. Thought it better to have a bit of a money cushion for an emergency fund when we got here, as I recall."

"We've definitely got ourselves an emergency," said Gerald. "But who'd have thought it would end up being gas?"

It was at that point the Captain began growling and fussing, until he was fairly spitting with frustration, in an effort to find something in his notebook. "Mah—Bo!" he finally sputtered out. "Mah—Bo!"

"Of course, it's your boat, my good man," the colonel replied, though he was too far across the table to clap him on the shoulder. "It will always be your boat, sir!"

"Mah—Bo—" He repeated louder and slower, reaching at the same time for his black marker.

Cole jumped to his feet (black being his color) and moved behind him to look over his shoulder. One, two, three vertical lines, and... an upside down M. Or, maybe it was a W. Then came an A, and eventually a T."

"Wah...watt..." Cole ran a hand through his wavy hair and concentrated harder. "Maybe he wants us to conserve water."

At which point the older man pulled his Captain's hat off and smacked his First Mate over the head with it.

"Cripes, Cap—give me another hint, then!"

"We could be getting low on water." Stella was thinking how much she enjoyed her evening shower. "Seems we haven't topped off since we were half-way through Canada."

"Not a problem," said Mason, "since we have the waterfall so close by."

"Wah—Fah!" the Captain thundered, with a resounding crash of his fist against the table that shook all their dishes.

"Waterfall!" Cole called it out as if it had been just before the buzzer in the game of Charades. "OK, waterfall. Geeze. What about it?"

Stuart flipped through his notebook then until he came to a very sketchy sketch that he shoved out into the center of the table for all of them to see.

"Reminds me of one of A.J.'s first wife's preliminary modern art sketches," Gerald mused, as they all stared at it. "The ones Lou got so much money for."

The Captain pointed at three parallel lines which looked similar to the three he had drawn on the table. He pulled Cole closer by the sleeve of his denim shirt, then thumped a spot on the paper that could have been a child's rendition of a sunshine face. The kind teacher's put on their papers for good work. "Mah—Bo," he insisted. Then smacked him on the shoulder, thumped the paper, again, and raised his voice. "Mah—Bo!"

They started building the "Mah-Bo," as it came to be called, the very next day.

8

After a great deal more deliberation the night before, Cole had suddenly recalled the Captain talking to him about alternative power systems and showing him a folder that was fairly bursting with articles cut out of magazines that he had been collecting for years. At the time, they had been discussing alternative fuels and the different modifications one would have to make to engines in order to even use them. However, a light went on when he remembered that incident, and he went down below to rifle through one of the shelves above Stuart's workbench to get the folder.

True to his guess, the Captain's face lit up, and it wasn't long before they found the blueprints for a homemade, electricity-producing, waterwheel. Something similar to what used to be seen on old mills. The way Stuart laughed (it was the first time since his episode) and kept repeating, "Mah-Bo!" and slapping Cole on the back half a dozen times, it was only natural that they should end up calling the contraption a Mah-Bo.

Once they knew what they were doing, everybody chipped in to help, and it was only a little over a week before the huge wheel was built, and the thing was operational. Mason had brought enough tools along to build a city. Of course, there were a few modifications that had to be made to run the wiring in and out of nearby trees, and over the fifty-foot span of water. But they now had their own power station that could produce all the electricity they would ever need. Including outside lights along the handrails of the bridge, that made it look like the entrance to a ride at *Disneyland.*

It was something that put even more of a cushion between them and the wild outside that surrounded them. In fact, very little had changed about their basic lifestyle since they had left *Villa Nofre*, the old Hollywood director's mansion in the beautiful Santa Ynez Mountains, back in California. The little group was actually discovering more opportunities in the unexpected situation, rather than setbacks.

Because of the increasing rain, any work area was fitted with a canopy of brown tarps. Soon, the side of the boat where damaged planks were being replaced, the after-deck, and the sawmill were crowned with them. Combined with the rope handrails that had been added to the boardwalk bridge (ever since Gerald had fallen halfway in when a foot slipped), the place was beginning to look like a movie set instead of a work area. Especially with the *Dreadnaught*, grounded on top of the rocks, like a shipwrecked pirate's vessel, rather than than the family's rambling home. Shipboard duties had long since given way to building improvements, and even the bell that had called all hands on deck, rang out primarily only at mealtimes.

They had even put together a three-sided wooden shelter (with a tarp on top) that faced their huge signal fire. Where those on fire watch could sit comfortably in deck chairs and stay dry. Stella found it amazing how a fire could be kept going in the rain. But as long as the wood was dry and it was burning hot enough, they could at least keep smoke going up in all but the heaviest downpours. Which was the important thing. Because once they got into the latter part of August, there seemed to be more rainy days than sunny ones.

Cole had ventured out a few times in the skiff, but so far he had never seen a single fishing boat. Too many small islands and rock outcroppings at the end of the cape that made working anywhere close to the area hazardous. But he still continued to try. He did come back with a beautiful forty-five pound halibut, the last time, though. Which, after a meal fit for royalty, Millie had packed the rest into the freezer, to be doled out through the coming weeks. It was after this feast that Stella and the colonel found themselves seated in the "fire hut" for the final watch of the day, that would last until sunset. An event that took place around eight-thirty, these days.

"Well, dearest," the colonel began as he poured them each a mug of hot chocolate from a tall metal thermos, "this isn't exactly how we expected to end our honeymoon. But it's an experience I'm sure we'll never forget."

"Even with the scary parts it's been the best experience I've ever had, Oliver. I think I could live through being stranded on the moon as long as you were there."

"I feel the same way, too, Stel. Being married to you is a delight I never expected to experience, at my age."

"Me, either." She blew gently on her chocolate and then tentatively took a sip. Delicious! "And wasn't it providential that Stuart got the others married before all this happened? He never would have been able to do that after his episode."

"Quite impossible. But you know I think that's half the reason everything's been going so smoothly for us, since. One always seems to feel more settled when they know things are done right."

"I agree. You know something?"

"What."

Stella breathed in the wonderful scent of campfire mingled with fresh air and pines, as she looked past the fire and out into the lovely meadow leading into the mountains, turning all gold in the setting sun. "I'm starting to like it so much here, I wouldn't really care if we never went on to the lodge. If you want to know the absolute truth about it... I don't feel the least bit lost, at all. Especially since Captain Stuart has something of an idea where we are, now."

"I've had the very same thoughts, myself." He set his cup down on the little table between them, and got up to put more wood on the fire. "I really think I've done my best work, here."

"I'm sure you have." She watched him pull a pair of work gloves out of his back pocket and put them on before hauling some of the brush and tree-trimmings they had cleared from the work areas, over to the waning flames. Funny how good physical work tended to make a person stronger rather than wearing them out. Especially if they enjoyed it. Not only was the colonel trimming down after all these weeks of adventuring, he was actually looking younger. Other than his wavy silver hair, but that just made him look distinguished. At least, that's what Stella was thinking, just then.

"You know, I wouldn't be all that disappointed if we never went back to civilization," he picked up the conversation as soon as he sat down, again. "Other than short business trips once or twice a year."

"That would be a lovely way to live, if you ask me." She suddenly lowered her voice to a whisper and pointed. "Oliver—look!"

In the far corner of the meadow a black bear was moving off into the trees. It was a wonderful moment, the two of them sharing the glimpse of a wild thing, going about its business as if they weren't there, at all.

"Do you think he sees us?" Stella asked.

"Oh, undoubtedly. But he's probably accepted that this is our territory now, so he'll keep his distance and stick to his. Seems they accept you if you give them half a chance and try to respect their space, as well."

"Mildred—put that gun down!" Mason's voice suddenly drifted across the water from the foredeck, where the two of them had also been watching the sunset.

"But I thought I saw something out there, Mase. I really did, this time!"

"We're just guests in this wilderness, so live and let live," he replied. "That's the new rule."

***

They say what one practices in their youth can never be surpassed by those who come to the same skill later in life. Such was evident in Daniel Boone (quoted at the beginning of this story), who began wandering through wilderness places on the edge of the Pennsylvania frontier, in his childhood. He received his first rifle by the age of twelve, and became (as other boys of his day) an essential contributor to the family food larder. After being persecuted in England for their dissenting beliefs, his parents (who were Quakers) emigrated to America in 1713, to join William Penn's colony. Daniel was the sixth of their eleven children.

Perhaps growing up in a large family, in a group known for their propensity to sacrifice themselves for others, is what laid the foundation for Daniel to become not only a provider and protector of his own, but other people, as well. However, having also been born during one of the most tumultuous times of American history—including the Indian wars and the Revolution—he was not destined for a life of peace.

Which is one of the things that makes him so unique. Because in spite of the many dangers, hardships and battles he faced throughout his life, he still managed—remarkably—to remain a man of strong morals, always willing to share with others, and a leader when it came to civic duties. He was elected three times to the Virginia General Assembly.

He is one of the first folk heroes of the United States, who became a legend in his own time. That unique position which comes from an admiring public who accepts the "tall tales" of a person's adventures right along with the true ones. Known best for forging and marking his famous Wilderness Road, through the Cumberland Gap in the Appalachian Mountains (that over 200,000 pioneers later used to find their way west), he is fondly remembered as the most colorful and extraordinary frontiersman the country has ever known. Respected for generations by friend and enemy alike, it is still commonly believed that if one knew even half what Daniel Boone did in his day, they could eventually find their way out of any wilderness they happened to fall into.

And I'm inclined to agree.

You can read more about this wonderful man—for free—over at:

http://www.gutenberg.org/files/46227/46227-h/46227-h.htm

To all those who who think they have nothing significant or worthwhile to offer—or that it's too late even if they did... may you know that it isn't.

THE LAST RESORT

A Stella Madison Caper

"To each there comes in their lifetime a special moment when they are figuratively tapped on the shoulder and offered the chance to do a very special thing, unique to them and fitted to their talents. What a tragedy if that moment finds them unprepared or unqualified for that which could have been their finest hour."

Winston Churchill

Stella Madison had been doing her morning exercise routine for so long she could do it without thinking. Which was exactly what she was up to that morning when the colonel interrupted her standing pushups to inform her that he had a "plot knot" to work out.

"Stel," he began before he even crossed the deck to stand beside her at the stern rail, "I've got the boys in something of a predicament. Are you up for a bit of brainstorming?"

"Of course, dear," she replied without even breaking her rhythm. "Two heads are better than one, I always say. Twelve, fourteen, fifteen! Set up the scene for me and I'll see if I can see something from a different angle."

"Excellent." He clapped his hands together and began to pace. "They've been in the cave for three days, now. So far, there's been no sign of—"

"Heavens..." she turned toward the mountain to starboard, kept a firm hold on the rail, and began her leg raises. "Are they lost?"

"Not at all, they're exploring. You see, it's imperative they find another way out before—"

"But wouldn't their parents worry? Thirteen, fifteen, sixteen... I mean, three whole days..."

"Oh, they aren't that young." He reached the port rail and turned to pace back in her direction, again. "Quite capable, really. Which is one of the main thrusts of the whole book." He jabbed at the air for example. "But you're right. Maybe I should emphasize it more at this point to keep that thought in the forefront."

"Especially for these difficult times we live in." She turned to face the mountain on their port side and continue with her other leg. "Seems like people are afraid of everything, nowadays."

"Right, again."

"You know, Oliver...(twenty-one, twenty-three, twenty-four...), as I've been reading along each day, I didn't get the feeling they were that old. Thirteen, or fourteen, is what I thought. That's how I've been picturing them, anyway. Twenty-five, twenty-eight, twenty-nine, thirty!" She flopped over from the waist, arched her back, and then slowly raised up, again, with a whisper of, "two, three!"

"Yes, they're in their early teens. I believe I even mentioned as much back at the beginning somewhere."

"I think young people are a lot more immature than we used to be at their age, don't you?"

"Definitely. That's part of the problem, of course. Being capable of so much more than they are actually allowed to do."

Stella flopped back down and began to come up slowly, again. "I couldn't agree more. Six, seven, eight!"

The colonel suddenly stopped and turned before he got to the opposite rail, this time. "Do you realize how many numbers you're skipping?"

"What?"

"Your counting, dearest. It's all over the place."

"Oh, that. Well, it doesn't matter so much. As long as I do six of each."

"Is there some reason why you don't just count to six and start over, again?"

"Not really. Except it wouldn't be half as encouraging as the higher numbers."

She knew by the way his silver eyebrows squeezed toward each other and his lower lip jutted out, that he didn't get the connection. But instead of arguing, or even trying to convince her to see things his way, he said, "Where were we?"

"In the cave." She began to run in place. Light, quick, bouncy steps. How wonderful it was to be married to a man who wasn't forever insisting she explain everything. "For three whole days!"

At which point there was a tremendous crash. The deck tipped at a crazy angle for a few seconds, followed by a resounding thud, and the two of them suddenly found themselves sliding on their backsides toward the lower rail. Without a thing they could do about it.

Stella screamed (she couldn't help it) at the same time she felt the colonel reach out and grab hold enough to keep her from tumbling over the side. Not that she hadn't always considered herself a fairly good swimmer. But this was Alaska! Where it was rumored one couldn't last much more than fifteen minutes in such cold water without slipping into something called hypothermia.

"Mason—Jeffries!" Millie bawled from the galley. "You just dropped my applesauce bread flatter than a pancake!" Stella saw her friend's auburn head come poking through a nearby porthole just as the colonel was helping her to her feet. "You're supposed to warn us before you do that kind of stuff!"

"I didn't do anything," the carpenter called back from across the little bridge that connected the *Dreadnaught* to the shore. "Been over here making lumber all morning." Then he came closer to look at the lopsided angle their ship was now tilted at. "What the... devil!"

A few minutes later, the door to the port companionway flung open and Millie's cousin, Gerald, staggered out with his orange life-jacket only hanging around his neck, and not tied. "Are we sinking?" He flung a look over the rail. "I say—there's a hole bigger than a garage door down below!"

"By the hoagie!" Mason hurried across the bridge, and Stella saw him automatically skip the three places where the slats were uneven, that tended to trip people. "How fast we got water coming in?"

"Well, that's the thing," Gerald pulled his black watch-cap off his head and ran a hand through his thin brown hair. "It isn't coming in at all, really. Just... pffft!" He demonstrated with a fist dangling over the rail. "Punched a big hole when we fell down onto the rocks. But we're still high and dry in that section. Pffft! Just like that." He demonstrated, again. "The two-foot lake we had down there, already, doesn't seem to be rising. Not sure we couldn't go slipping off the rocks, though, at this angle."

All at once, the ship's bell began to tap out two beats and a pause, two beats and a pause, from up in the wheelhouse where the Captain had been enjoying his morning coffee.

"Oh, my word—Captain Stuart—" Stella was still hanging onto the colonel's strong arm to steady herself. "I can't imagine how he could even stand up on this slant."

"We've stopped moving, at least," said the colonel. "I

better go check on him."

It was at that moment they saw Cole, their dark-haired First Mate, sprinting down the hillside path from the waterfall in response to his personal signal from the bell. His wife, Lou Edna, appeared a few minutes later, picking her way more carefully since she had the Senator (not quite a year old) packed into the shoulder carrier she was wearing. By the time a close inspection had been made by all aboard (the Captain had been hefted onto Cole's back in a fireman's carry, in order to avoid all the steps down through the companionways), the true culprit responsible for the morning's incident had been discovered.

"Dry rot!" Mason slogged back through the knee-deep water, to the little group that was gathered where the deck was still high enough to be dry. He held out a chunk of the spongy wood to prove his point. "If we got it here, we got it in other places, too. Collapsed right where we hammered in the braces, when we first got here. Couldn't hold up under the pressure."

There was a long sobering silence as they all thought about this for awhile.

"So, our original plan of firing up the engine and getting ourselves off these rocks in the spring," said the colonel, "is now no longer possible."

"Not without rebuilding most of the hull, it isn't," Mason agreed.

"How long would that take?" Gerald asked. He still had the orange life-jacket hanging around his neck. In case he should happen to slip down that steep incline and out through the hole, as he had whispered aside to Stella.

"Better part of a year, at least." Mason rubbed a hand over his stubble of salt-and-pepper whiskers. "That's if we all pitched in. Full time. Maybe even more."

"I can't do a whole year!" Lou Edna objected as she subconsciously reached back to disentangle her blonde ponytail from her little son's inquisitive fingers. "This baby's due in February and I gotta have drugs! I am not—repeat—not—going through what I did last time!"

"Not to mention the state old Stuart could be in," Gerald reminded everyone, "if he doesn't get some serious medical. As soon as possible, too, because—"

The gray-haired captain thumped him with his wooden walking stick, but it only bounced off the life-jacket and didn't hit home. Gerald flinched and stepped out of range, taking care not to slip down the incline. The old man was sitting on one of the many boxes that made up the mountain of supplies they had brought along to move into Mason's lodge in Alaska. The one he had won in a card game over ten years ago, and never seen. But there was no doubt it was still there, since he had faithfully been keeping up on the tax bills that were sent to him every year. Should he ever want to trade it off, again. Except nobody ever seemed to want it. Which was a good thing. The economy being what it was, his own family needed it, now.

Seeing the captain seated so comfortably in that particular spot, Stella thought how much he had improved since his "episode" (as they called it). He spent quite a bit of time fishing down here in their "Two Foot Lake," once Cole got him situated every afternoon. Ever since he discovered the inside pond was an attraction for several varieties of fish that came in with the tide. Particularly during storms. With Millie keeping him in good supply of coffee and sandwiches, it was a kind of therapy all by itself. At least his outbursts of frustration (at not being able to speak) were fewer and farther between. However, she did agree with Gerald, that one should never allow themselves to resort to blows just because others couldn't understand them. Even more so if they had temper.

Now, he reached into his shirt pocket where he had several colored marking pens and took out the black one. It was the First Mate's color, who—being ever attentive to his captain when they were in close proximity to each other—stepped up beside the older man and waited as he began to spell something out on the little whiteboard he carried around. The one that used to hang in the pantry so Millie could keep track of supplies.

"E...N...in what? S..." The captain swung the whiteboard at him, but the young man had long since stopped standing too close while Stuart was painstakingly trying to spell out letters with an inadequate left hand. "Forget that one. What's next? I...D... inside?" Another swipe. "I mean, N... E...that's it? Cripes, Cap, that doesn't spell anything."

The captain smeared off the bottom of the S with the end of his finger, and added a tail. Then underlined it.

"G," Cole murmured. "Engine! Engine? The engine's good. Didn't even come close to the the engine."

At which point Stuart threw the whiteboard at him.

Cole caught it in midair and handed it back to him. "Give me something else, then. Geeze. I'm not a mind reader. "B...A...C...back? We'd sink if I backed her up. You know that. What next—Y...A ...R...backyard! Man, we don't have a backyard."

"Mah—Bo!" They were the only two words the man could articulate, and—up to that point—had always referred to the waterwheel they built up at the falls to make their electricity. Which was the ultimate in frustration considering the fact the man was an amateur inventor, who used to take great delight in explaining the inner workings of all things mechanical to anyone who would listen. Something he and his First Mate had passed many hours doing before the episode (some sort of stroke) robbed him of the use of half his body, including his tongue. But his mind was still sharp as ever.

Ten minutes and many charades later, Cole was headed to the workshop area beside the engine room to rummage through a shelf of books and manuals for one called, *Backyard Boats Book*. And considering the last time he did this had resulted in building the waterwheel, they were fairly certain their captain was trying to direct them in the most practical way to make necessary repairs to the *Dreadnaught*. Which was only partly right.

He wanted them to build another boat, entirely.

It was a small, squat-looking thing that resembled more of a tugboat than a motor-cruiser. However, the plans (included in the *Backyard Boats Book*) were amazingly simple. Something about being built from the "chine" method, which required no complicated bending of the wood. Anywhere. In fact, Mason calculated they could actually have such a project completed—and ready to launch—before Christmas.

In spite of its looks, it would be well-balanced and seaworthy. The one drawback was that all working systems would have to be scavenged from the *Dreadnaught*, making it fairly probable that the old ship would never get off the rocks, again. At least, not without investing much more than she was worth to make it happen. A thought that sent a wave of remorse through the family, since it had been their only home for so many months, now.

That, and the fact the new boat would only be large enough for three.

Of course, there was no question about who would go. The two who needed medical attention and the only able-bodied seaman among them who could handle a boat in the rough coastal waters of winter. The rest would have to stay with the *Dreadnaught.* At least long enough for their "forward group" to get whatever medical help they needed, then locate the abandoned lodge they had been headed for in the first place. Who knew if it was even livable enough to move into? It was a mission that could take anywhere from a week, to a month, or even longer. Depending on where the group landed.

It was a dangerous undertaking, no matter how Stella looked at it, but no one was talking about that part. Although she was certain everyone was thinking about it. Even more since Lou Edna had declared her intentions to take the Senator (the name she had given her son so he would have some advantage in life) along with them. The young woman's reasoning being that she trusted Cole enough to paddle them to safety on a surfboard, if he had to. So, that was that. It was a point the others might have argued against and prevailed. Except those left behind might even be worse off, should there be some reason they were never rescued, at all.

A fact which rested heavier on Millie, each day, as she watched the *Mah-Bo II* taking shape, right before her eyes. Once they had set up another covered work area (so large it blocked out their former view of the waterfall from the galley porthole), the men had been working feverishly on the new project, every day. Almost as if they knew something the women didn't. At least, that's what Stella was thinking as she and Millie were having a cup of tea while they were on fire-watch, some five weeks after construction began.

"Funny we're almost through October, and it doesn't seem half as cold as when we first got here." Stella stirred a squirt of lemon juice into her tea, along with a spoon of brown sugar. "You think we're getting used to the weather? Or it's maybe just another sign of global warming."

"Definitely global warming." Millie held her cup between her hands and blew gently on it before taking a sip. "Wouldn't surprise me if the whole northwest didn't feel the same as California in the next ten years. If they don't blow up the planet before then."

"I thought you said only part of it would get blown up. Otherwise what's the point of collecting so much food for? You've got enough in your famine chest to last ten years, already. What with the way you've been packing away fish and canning berries."

"Depends on how many people you end up having to share with. Seems I collect people the same way furniture collects dust."

Stella laughed at that because it was so true. Especially since she had to admit she was one of those "dust people," herself. She and Millie had gone over many end-of-the-world scenarios on this trip. It was one of the subjects she could always count on to get a good conversation going when one was desperately needed. Like now. Except just when she would have been perfectly content to let Millie sail into her favorite subject, and out of the swamps of despair that had been coming on, Stella was suddenly struck with a most brilliant idea. She gasped, set her cup down on the wood stump between their two deck chairs, and jumped to her feet.

"What!" Millie sprang to her feet, too, and began fumbling out of her leather work gloves to unzip her jacket and get at her gun. "Oh, dear God—is it a bear?"

"No, of course not. I haven't seen one this close since you fired off that first shot and we started keeping the signal fire. "It's just that—"

"Stel, you almost gave me another heart attack!"

"Well, it caught me off guard."

"What did."

"The *Dreadnaught*. Sitting there like some big hulking elephant with a broken leg."

"But it's looked like that for ages, now." Millie sighed and sat down in her chair, again. "It's one of the things that's so depressing about all this. Even shored up to level, again, it looks like some ramshackle tenement building in downtown L.A. I've never had to live so low in my life—I never have. I'm not cut out for it. Every improvement Mason adds onto it—for our comfort, he says—makes it look worse and worse." She picked up her tea, again. "He used to do beautiful work back at the *Villa Nofre*. He's just in too big a hurry, here. Never takes time to finish anything."

"That's the idea I had this very minute, Millie. Why don't you and I finish it?"

"Me? I couldn't hammer a nail straight if you paid me."

"Not the carpentry part. The painting part. Let's paint the whole thing from top to bottom. Just think how much better it will make everyone feel."

"Well... it would definitely give me something else to do besides knitting one sock over and over to settle my nerves." She pursed her lips together for a moment and thought about it. "There's plenty of paint, too. Did you notice how many cans Stuart had to drag out of the pantry just to get all our food in?"

"I certainly did."

"That's all that was in there was paint. Most of it in those big five-gallon cans, too."

"Paint, paint, and more paint."

"Let's do it."

A resolve that lost a bit of enthusiasm, later on, when they realized there were only three colors in all those cans. Black, white, and a rather rusty red color that had something of a metallic smell to it. However, their spirits rose, again, when they realized how much better things would look with a fresh coat of anything on the outside cabin areas (which hadn't been painted in so long they were grease-stained and gray), and over the new wooden additions Mason had enclosed several of the decks with. Living in a rainforest had made it necessary to add more covered areas.

Since nearly a third of the outside decks on the starboard side of the ship had now been turned into a greenhouse (something that went a long way toward making Gerald's cabin look less like a jungle, and actually brought him out into the sun more often), and the entire stern deck had been screened in with netting to keep out mosquitoes, their comfort levels had risen considerably. Not to mention the addition to the wheelhouse on the upper deck, that nearly tripled the space where Stuart lived, since he moved out of the chief engineer's cabin, next to the engine room. Now, he had large windows on three sides, and could see for miles all around. Right from his comfortable leather chair behind the wheel. He even had a door to the outside decks. Comforts, indeed!

Something that made Stella wonder if the captain had any idea how much better he had things, out in this wilderness, than if he were jammed into some rehab center with hundreds of other people. Not that Gerald wasn't right about him needing therapy—he had a temper like a hornet, and about as much patience as a wet cat. But it seemed to her that he was steadily improving as the days went by. Even more so since he had been using the walking stick. Why, he hadn't had a major blow-up in weeks. Which is why it came as such a surprise when he discovered what she and Millie had been doing with his paint. If he could have got only one word out that was understandable... she was sure it would have been a swear word.

Their only salvation was that they could outrun him.

4

It was Cole who finally settled things when he explained that the rust-colored "bottom paint" was mixed with copper to ward off sea-growth (and other living things) from attaching to the wood. It was extremely expensive. In fact, it was actually one of the reasons their hull had begun to rot in the first place. The Captain had not painted the *Dreadnaught*'s bottom in nearly five years. He was on a fixed income since he retired and it had taken that long just to collect enough of the stuff to cover such a large area. That and to save up for the expense of hauling a vessel that size (eighty feet long) out of the water and into a commercial yard to do it.

None of which had happened before they embarked on their long voyage.

In the end, the women apologized (even though Stuart should have been the one to apologize for chasing them with a walking stick) and reluctantly agreed to use only the black, or white. And, of course, the fifteen gallons of "taupe" they had concocted by mixing all three colors together. And while Stuart only agreed on that point because it was ruined for bottom paint after diluting so much, he still grumbled every time they brought it out to paint the trim.

"Oh, he'll get over it," Millie reasoned, "when he sees how much better it looks after we're done. I just wish we could work faster. A grouch in the crowd is like having a rotten potato in the bin. It only takes one to make the whole place smell."

That's when Stella came up with the idea of using a mop, instead of brushes and rollers for the larger areas. Something that proved way too exhausting because of the weight (even with the strings cut short), until Lou Edna pitched into the project and took over that part. Leaving the other two to the more artistic job of painting on trim in places where there wasn't any. Which is how it came to be that such things as shutters and a bit of Victorian Era "gingerbread" began to appear in various spots, making the vessel look more like a floating hotel, instead of a boat.

A transformation that so appealed to the ladies, they even painted a fancy sign to hang off the stern rail (where Stuart couldn't see it, but anyone who might come into their inlet would) with the words *"The Last Resort"* painted on. Then, in smaller letters underneath, *"Visitors Welcome."* By the time they were finished, and had even decorated with potted ferns gathered from the woods (some hanging, and some set out on the decks) it actually began to take on the atmosphere of a wonderfully unique vacation spot rather than a shipwreck.

Something that not only went a long way toward lifting Millie's spirits, but everyone else's, besides. Including Captain Stuart's. Whose new favorite place turned out to be a little covered area outside the wheelhouse (decorated with deck furniture and potted ferns), where he could supervise the construction of the

Mah-Bo II from all angles, without having to so much as leave his chair.

The new boat was set up on skids that would allow it to slide right down into the water when it was ready to launch. An event that happened at sunrise, sometime around the middle of November, on a particularly clear, still, day before the first snow. The crew of three (and a half) did not want to run into heavy seas before they got away from the rocks and out into the middle of the strait. A place they at least hoped the weather channels would start coming in again on the radio, and they would be able to take some proper bearings.

The colonel said a prayer of blessing over them all, and—after a few brief hugs—the *Mah-Bo II* chugged out of the inlet under the power of the *Dreadnaught*'s cleaned-up engine, fitted out with new hoses, filters, and anything else they could replace from what they had spares for. The little craft looked stout and nautical. Especially with its black hull, white cabin top, and two coats of that expensive bottom paint below the waterline (which couldn't be seen, but it was a comfort just knowing it was there). And even though they all agreed it was better not to drag out such times...

It was a sad parting.

Gerald smoothed down his mustache and then jammed his hands into his coat pockets. "Well, I better go check the temperature in my greenhouse... or, something."

"Let's set on another pot of coffee." Mason put a comforting arm around Millie, who had rivers of silent tears streaming down her face as she watched half her family slip out of sight.

"Stella and I brought ours in the thermos," said the colonel. "Thought it might be good to start the signal fire early, today."

Which is how it happened that everyone drifted off into different places in order to get over those first few hours of almost unbearable emptiness that comes from loved ones having to depart under questionable circumstances. Even Stella and the colonel—who never lacked for subjects to talk about—found it difficult to make light conversation. Instead, she sat in one of the deck chairs under the three-sided fireside shelter and watched him build and light the fire. In no particular hurry.

To tell the truth, it was all she could do to keep from thinking about that toddler, as happy and bouncy as he always was, looking more adorable than ever in his yellow slicker, rain hat, and rubber boots. A miniature version of the foul-weather gear fisherman wore. Oh, she missed him, already!

"Well, dearest," the colonel finally sat down in the chair next to her as the fire began to crackle and roar, "I have a confession to make."

"I can't imagine what it would be, Oliver. You're about the most perfect person I've ever known."

Which gave him a small chuckle and he reached across to take hold of her hand. "Love is blind, as the saying goes."

"Rather a nice handicap, if you ask me."

"Never-the-less, I think it only fair to apologize for making decisions which could possibly lead us to having to spend the rest of our lives here."

"Seems I remember we all had a vote in that," she

reminded him, "and it was unanimous, too. But, dear, you don't—" Stella felt a sudden catch in her throat and had to wait a few seconds before she could even speak the words. "You're not saying you think they won't make it, are you? Because I couldn't bear that. Oh, why did we even let them—"

"Not in the least, not in the least." He gave her hand a squeeze for emphasis. "On the contrary, I'm more impressed with that boat than I ever thought I could be. Turned out surprisingly well."

"What then. The weather?"

"I think even if they do hit bad weather it'll bear up fine enough to allow them to run into a cove somewhere and wait it out. No..." He sighed a heavy sigh. "It's nothing to do with the boat or their capabilities. It's—"

A piece of kindling burned through and sent a larger stick of wood tumbling from the pile. The colonel paused long enough to get up and pick up another one to push it back into the flames, again. "No, it's the possibility we might have set them up with the opportunity to..." He returned to his seat. "Abscond with everything we've got and, um... never tell a living soul we're out here."

Stella gasped. They had all turned over debit cards and lists for things they needed to be brought back (what with the holidays and all). "But Oliver—dear! It was you who suggested it. You even handed yours over, first. Now you're having second thoughts?"

"No, not second thoughts. I knew right off it would be a difficult temptation for Lou. At the same time, I also knew she needed to feel the depth of our belief in the changes she's made. Trusting her, it seemed to me, would have the biggest impact. Anyway, I saw the chance and took it. Which I shouldn't have done—I only just now realized—without consulting you. And everyone else, as well."

There was a long silence (she couldn't help it, she was shocked).

"That said, I should probably also tell you this isn't the first time I've made such hasty, ill-thought -out decisions. I've made them all my life. It's one of the reasons my first wife divorced me and married someone else." He sighed, again. "There. Better to have all that out in the open, than to go on letting you think I'm so perfect. I really don't know why everyone in this family believes I have the answers to everything. I never did. And I'm not some prophet with a personal line to God's ear, either. Nobody is."

Stella thought for a few moments, breathed in the fragrant woodsmoke, and then looked out across the meadow to where the sunlight was just beginning to touch the tops of the far-off forest. It occurred to her just then that she actually loved it here. "You know something, Oliver?"

"Whatever you think, I won't blame you. No doubt about that."

"What I think is... this might be just the right time to tell you why my driver's license says I'm eighty-two, instead of sixty-three."

"Whatever the reason, I can't still blame you," the colonel insisted. "Not now. Not knowing the way you are and loving you so much for it."

A statement that went a long way in giving Stella the courage to tell. "Well, it's a story that goes back a long time. So, I guess I should start at the beginning."

"Always best to start at the beginning," he agreed. "Always."

"All right, then." Now, it was her turn to take a deep breath, and she took one before plunging in.

"I was raised in the most wonderful, fun-loving family, Oliver," she began. "I really was. My parents were both teachers and they loved each other immensely. They married late in life and I was their only child."

"I knew that delightful optimism had to come from somewhere," he replied. "Go on."

"Well, with a childhood surrounded by books and so much enthusiasm for the pleasures of learning, I ended up following the teaching profession, too."

"Only natural."

"Yes, I suppose. Anyway, by the time I graduated college and got my first contract—teaching English at the *Harristown School for Girls*, in Pennsylvania—my parents were getting on in years and I decided to move back in with them."

"Also quite natural." He opened the picnic basket they had brought out earlier and took out two mugs and the thermos. "Cream and sugar, this morning?"

"I'd love cream and sugar, this morning. I just might have cream and sugar from now on."

"Under the circumstances, I think it's a fine idea. Might as well enjoy ourselves. So, you moved back in with your parents. Then what."

"Then my Aunt Mad—she was my father's younger sister, and our only living relative—went back to Broadway. She had been living with them while I was away at school, and teaching drama at the Harristown School, too. But she missed the real theater."

"A true actress, then."

"Only in small supporting roles. But you know they kept her busy all the time? She was quite a character in real life, too. I was named after her. And I loved her very much." Stella felt another catch in her throat (what an emotional morning it had been!) and waited for it to pass. "She gave me everything she had."

"I suppose you inherited, later. Being her only family."

"You could say that." She blew on her coffee and took a sip. "She was married once but it was way before I came along. Her husband died in the war. World War II, it was. He was a navigator on a B-17 bomber. Anyway, she never married, again. She was the eccentric old aunt like you read about in books. That's why we called her Aunt Mad. Although it was really short for Madison. Now, I'm going to skip ahead, because absolutely nothing happened for the next twenty something years."

"Nothing at all?"

"Nothing to do with the story. Anyway, the years went by. First my father passed away and then—not even a year later—my mother."

"Often happens when people are close."

"I've heard that, too, and that's just how it was. Well, for the first time in my life I was all alone in the world. You can't count college because no one's really alone there. Always somebody around. But after Mom died, too, I was so despondent. I knew I needed a complete change."

"Understandable."

"So, I packed everything up and went to New York, to live with Aunt Mad. Who was in her late sixties by then but still taking on a few roles just to keep herself in shape. She was always dedicated to staying in shape."

"Ah, that's where you get those tendencies."

"Goodness, she had me doing morning exercises since I was twelve."

"It shows."

"Thank you, dear. It wasn't difficult. I admired her and always wanted to be like her. But it was truly providence that I moved in. I can see that now, looking back on it. Because less than a year later, she was diagnosed with heart disease and I ended up taking care of her the way I had my parents. You know, when you live with someone that has an illness, your life becomes enmeshed with doctor's appointments and hospital stays. Not much time for anything else."

"Lonely, too, I imagine."

Stella realized he knew where she was going with all this, and probably even knew how much she was avoiding the actual point. Then it occurred to her (funny how a person's mind can jump ahead to conclusions at the very time they're busy doing something else) that Colonel Oliver P. Henry knew her as well, if not better, than she knew herself. At least as thoroughly as she had come to know him. Which was her favorite, all-consuming pastime, these days. Getting to know him. At which point, such a feeling of love washed over her for this man she had married, that the rest of the story came out all in a rush. Practically without thinking.

"Oliver? I married the most wonderful man in the world—that I knew nothing about—who turned into the most horrid man in the world, not two months after I married him. He was either a spy, or insane. I don't know which. He actually tried to kill me—twice!"

"Stella!" The way he whispered it, along with the look on his face, indicated he was thinking of never having met her rather than how she could have possibly made such an error in judgment.

It was the only thing that gave her courage to get to the hard part. Because all those old dredged-up emotions were now beginning to churn inside her like the rumble of thunder before a storm. "He was terrible to Aunt Mad, too," she pressed on.

"So, I... I had to put her in a home until I could straighten things out. Except I never did get things straightened out. They only got worse and worse. I even had to take a leave of absence from my job and move. In the middle of the school year! But he followed me. Next I tried moving out of state. But he found me that time, too. I don't know how. I actually think he was trying to drive me crazy. For my savings, maybe. Not that I had so much, but I lived a simple life and did have a small inheritance from my parents. By that time, I was close to a nervous breakdown. I'm almost sure of it."

"Did you ever go to the police?"

"I couldn't make myself. He was always threatening to kill Aunt Mad if I did. Then he got more reasonable for a time—probably because I'd moved her around so much by then, he couldn't find her. Anyway, he said if I turned over my savings..."

"Oh, Stel."

"He'd at least give me a divorce and leave us alone. Of course, he didn't. I got the divorce, though. Because I didn't turn over any money until it went through. But..." She set her cup down on the wood block and looked out at the meadow, again. There were three black-tailed deer grazing out there, now. "It wasn't long until he wanted Aunt Mad's money, too. And she had quite a lot."

"You should have gone to the police. Seems you both would have been prime candidates for a witness protection program."

"But I couldn't prove anything. Other than incompatibility and there's no law against that. He was very cunning. Almost like a politician. Only worse. Anyway, one day, I woke up with the most urgent feeling that I should move Mad, again. Just as fast as I possibly could. You know, I wonder if that came from the Lord." She looked back at the colonel. "Do you think God intervenes in people's lives that way, even before they become Christians? I know he does afterward. I believe that with all my heart."

"Most definitely. He knows our end from the beginning. Who will choose him, and who won't. I'm sure all believers can look back on times when someone—or something—intervened at a vital point in their lives before they ever knew him."

"I think so, too. And it definitely explains a lot of things to look at it that way. Like my hair turning prematurely white before the age of fifty."

"Indeed. So, did you get Aunt Mad moved then?"

"She wouldn't go. She was scheduled to have her

pacemaker replaced the following week, and felt she'd be perfectly safe in the hospital until she recovered. Instead, she came up with another idea. A brilliant one, actually. Except... it backfired on us."

"She wasn't really mad, you know," Stella insisted. "Just eccentric. Had her own ideas about things."

"Nothing wrong with that," the colonel agreed.

"But she was independent, too. Didn't like being told what to do. Having to be shuffled from one facility after the other in such a short time... well, it was definitely taking a toll on her. The poor dear wasn't well to begin with. You know, Oliver? Sometimes I think people get misdiagnosed with Alzheimer's when it's only a reaction to some drug they're taking. Or maybe even a temporary response to a bad situation at an age when they're not up to handling that kind of stress, anymore. Sort of a defense mechanism, you might say."

"I wouldn't be surprised."

"I've thought a lot about it." Stella held her cup out for a warm-up when the colonel opened the thermos, again. "I never for a minute believed she had Alzheimer's." She was quiet for a long time after that. Just sipping on her coffee and thinking back over it all.

"I take it you had a more difficult time getting her back out of those places than into them."

"I certainly did. Except..."

"Except?"

"Except it was me that couldn't get out, Oliver. Because we switched places."

"Stella!" The coffee he was pouring into his own cup spilled over the brim, onto his hand, and he nearly dropped it before setting the thermos down. But he barely noticed. "What were you—how could you even—"

"It was Aunt Mad, dear. She was so convincing. Which was one of her gifts. You know what she said?"

"I'd like to know what she said. Indeed, I would!" He switched his cup to the other hand and shook the spilled coffee off his other one. "You're a very reasonable woman, as a rule. I can't imagine you'd be taken in by such a thing. Or that something like that was even possible to pull off. Not for any length of time, anyway."

Which Stella couldn't reply to because she didn't know the answer to that, either.

"What exactly did she say?"

"She said, Stella, my girl? This... could very well be... our finest hour!"

"That's it?"

"Well, then she went into one of her long stories about surviving the World War. How Churchill kept saying everyone was going to be tapped on the shoulder at some point—figuratively speaking—and called upon to do something only they were perfectly skilled in, or had the talent for. That we should all be working to perfect our skills and talents for just such a time. What could be worse, he said, than not being up to it at the moment your time came. You would miss your finest hour. Or some such thing. I forget exactly how it went. Except I've been looking for my finest hour ever since."

Now the colonel was quiet for so long she had to glance over to make sure he didn't think she might be crazy, after all. That thing she had been afraid of all along, and the reason she hadn't been brave enough to tell him she had spent so much time in a mental institution in the first place. Which suddenly made her wonder if such an omission might be grounds for divorce.

She began to get butterflies.

"Dearest!" It was as if everything had come clear to him, all at once. He set his cup down, then hers, so he could take both of her hands in his own. "To spend one's life looking for their finest hour... I can't think of anything more noble!"

"But I've never had one, Oliver," Might as well be up front with it all because she couldn't take another session like this one, again. The thought of losing the happiest times in her life over her mistakes of the past was practically unbearable. "I've failed miserably at everything I've ever tried." She came right out and admitted it.

"Don't tell me your ex-husband found you, again, after all that."

"No. But I had nightmares about the possibility for the rest of my life. Not to mention a phobia about getting home before dark, every night."

"Then—in spite of the dire consequences—the brilliant plan worked. Did it not?"

"Not really, because I lost my Aunt Mad. Entirely. I Never did see her, again. And because we had done such a terribly good job of switching places—my white hair and all—we could have been twins! Can you believe that? And she was so sure they would let me out a few days later, after preliminary blood tests for the surgery. When our blood type didn't match. Then I was supposed to explain how she had tricked me. She told me to blame everything on her since it was going to be her finest hour. She wanted to do it up right, she said. And she was sure they'd believe it because she'd been pulling things like that over on them for quite a while, anyway."

A twinkle came into the colonel's eye but he kept a straight face.

"You know, she snuck out more than once to see a Broadway show? Right under their noses! They don't watch people half well enough in those places."

"So, even if they didn't believe you, why wasn't it just as easy for you to walk out? And I can't imagine the hospital didn't release you the very minute they found out you were the wrong person."

"Because there never was a surgery scheduled. It was only the story they told her so she'd go peacefully while being transferred to a lock-down ward at the, um... state hospital."

The colonel gasped.

"For hard-to-handle Alzheimer's patients."

"But—good heavens—what about the blood type?"

"She was my father's sister. And, I'm afraid, it turned out we had the same blood type, too."

"Stella—dearest! How long did they keep you in for?"

"Two years. It took that long to quell my temper, and stop acting like a crazy person. I think I really was temporarily out of my mind. I was that upset."

"I don't blame you."

"But I had to behave normal enough for them to even

begin to listen to me. It was the only way. Something extremely difficult to do under heavy sedation. You know they drug everybody in those places?

"I can't imagine."

"Not everyone to the same extent but they do. Even more so at eight o'clock"

"Eight o'clock?"

"PM. The bedtime hour. There's no such thing as insomnia in a place like that. Especially if you can't behave."

"My word. I do some of my best work during bouts of insomnia."

"A lot of older people do. But you can't do it there. It's practically impossible to do anything there, really, except the most basic of human functions. Simply because you feel like a zombie most of the time. But I finally made friends with a young aide, who helped me a great deal."

"Another divine intervention!"

"I think so. Little Clarita Alverez. She helped me track down the last remaining shreds of my paper trail. The one I tried so hard to erase for three years before that, so you-know-who wouldn't find me, again. And because all my current documentation disappeared with Aunt Mad... well, I had to locate enough witnesses, who could remember me and go to court. But you know how long the court system takes."

"What about duplicate driver's license's—passports —that sort of thing?"

"The name Stella Madison always bounced back to Aunt Mad. Who was recorded to have died of heart disease, the same year all this happened. But I don't for a moment believe that. In fact, I wouldn't put it past her to try covering her tracks—my tracks, I mean—thinking she was doing me a favor, before she even got to the apartment in California. The one I had already rented for us there, where we agreed to meet. Then again, she might have just taken off on her own. As much as she loved me, I think she'd had quite enough of rest homes by then. Not to mention her finest hours."

The colonel was quiet, just trying to take it all in. But he still had hold of her hands, so Stella was encouraged by that. In fact, she felt as if a great burden had been lifted off her. Why hadn't she told him sooner?

"You know, dearest," he spoke thoughtfully, "if we ever get back to civilization, I'd like to try and look into this a little, myself. I've had to do a lot of people-searching in my profession, and I don't mind saying I'm pretty good at it."

"Well, if you'd like to, dear."

"I would. After everything you've been through, it would at least put your mind at ease knowing what really happened."

"It certainly would."

"What is your real name, then. The one you traded off to Aunt Mad."

"Stella Madison."

"What?"

"Stella Madison, dear. She was my father's sister, and I was named after her. I thought I told you that, already."

Millie had a turkey for Thanksgiving. In fact, she had brought three—who knew how far the nearest grocery store would be when living in the wilds of Alaska? Little did any of them know how literal that situation would become. At any rate, when the holiday finally rolled around, their meal lacked nothing that might be found on millions of other American tables for that special day. Some things were even better.

For instance, the cranberry sauce was made fresh, from a patch of berries Lou Edna had discovered at the far end of the meadow, just where the muskeg began. It was a beautiful spot near the edge of the forest, that led to a piece of land which had the most sunlight of any place in the tiny valley. Because it was directly in the path of sunrise as it came spilling in over the rocky coast, every morning. Before bumping into the mountains that ran along each side of their narrow inlet.

It wasn't until the little family had gone, and the rest of them took a picnic to see if there might still be enough of a crop left to can, that they discovered the beginnings of a cabin near the place. Which might have been exciting (the prospect of other people living somewhere close by!), if evidence hadn't pointed to it simply being a project of their two youngest family members. The tools laying about were marked, *Dreadnaught*, and all the lumber had been carried over from Mason's sawmill. So, the young couple was simply building a nest of their own. And doing quite the nice job of it, too.

Less than a week later, it began to snow.

Huge silent flakes floated down in the morning, and by late afternoon, there was already a blanket of white everywhere. As temperatures dropped and activities began to shrink to inside projects, where it was warmer, Stella had a feeling she would like this season most of all. The loveliness from every window, the coziness of the wood stoves, and the wonderful closeness that came from everyone working and enjoying themselves, together.

Even Gerald, who had long since lost the cut-off serape he had worn constantly to keep himself warm, had become stronger and more tanned after weeks of working outside on the *Mah-Bo II*. Of course, it could have also had something to do with not taking thirty pills every day, too. He had stopped doing that after their last storm at sea, when he couldn't keep anything down for over three days. Only to discover he hadn't felt so good in years. Which, as often happens in such cases, led from one good thing to another. It started with him wanting to move some of his larger plants outside during their dormant season.

Something the colonel ended up helping with, not only because he needed something physical to do after spending so many hours writing at his desk every day, but because Stuart's enthusiasm for growing things was contagious. It was the reason the colonel's rooftop garden at the *Villa Nofre* was so abundant when Stella first met him. Not to mention the many little wooden pots and planter boxes that were lined up in front of their bank of French windows, and tucked into various nooks and crannies all over their living quarters, even now.

Then there was the matter of having to enclose the area with wire and fence in order to keep the deer away. A project that had particular appeal to Mason, who had run out of things to do inside already, and liked to stay busy. So it was that a routine developed among them, where the men went outside to work every afternoon (being retired, they liked their slow mornings), while Stella and Millie continued the latest development of a project of their own. It was a cookbook offering famous recipes from *The Last Resort*, that they could sell to tourists who enjoyed their stay here.

If they ever got any.

Having come to Alaska to run a lodge, they decided to ignore the fact they were still shipwrecked. At the moment (the first clear day after an entire week of snow) they were too happily engrossed in trying to take the perfect picture of a freshly baked Huckleberry Betty for the cover, to even think about setbacks.

The light coming in through the large porthole above the sink counter in the galley suddenly glowed beautifully down onto the red ceramic baking dish (maybe they should add a sprig of evergreen and put it in the holiday section), and Stella snapped several angles of it. Just to get things right. Then, as they had their heads together and were clicking silently through the preview slides to decide which was best, they began to hear the far-off drone of a motor.

"Stuart and the kids!" Millie nearly knocked over the little bowl of whipped cream they had set next to the dessert (for added appeal), just trying to get to her jacket that was hanging near the door. "They actually came back!"

Which made Stella realize she and the colonel weren't the only ones who had been worried about putting such temptation in front of their former house thief. Especially since they had passed the three-week mark, denoting the earliest they might possibly expect them to return. But it didn't turn out to be the rest of their family, after all. As the noise of an engine increased, and the two of them stood out in front of the wheelhouse, looking around in all directions...

They finally spotted a lone snow machine heading toward them on its way through the pass.

They were saved!

At the very least, they were saved! No matter who it turned out to be, there were other people living on this very island who could get them back in touch with civilization. Which led to a royal welcome—a bit overwhelming to the bewildered visitors—when the motor finally shut down and two bundled up riders climbed off in front of the bridge.

"What is this-place?" said a female voice, pulling off her helmet at the same time, and letting loose a waterfall of long black hair. "Sammy, look at this-place! It looks like a—a—"

"A hotel!" Millie finished for her. "Welcome to *The Last Resort*! That's the name of it. Come on in for some coffee and Huckleberry Betty. Fresh out of the oven."

"We didn't bring any money, though," said a man,

dressed in camouflage, with a rifle slung across his back. He also had a cascade of black hair, but it only fell to his shoulders when he took off his helmet. "Just out for some hunting. We come every year. Can't get here unless it snows."

"Oh, it's on the house. Right, Stella?"

"Of course it is. We're so happy to see people, we're hoping you'll stay for supper, too. Here come the men, they must have heard you drive up."

At which point, the colonel, Mason, and Gerald appeared at the head of the path to the waterfall, where they had been running more wires for electricity out to Gerald's new potting shack.

"By the hoagie—if this isn't Christmas come early!" Mason gave the man a friendly smack on the shoulder. "Where did you come from, boy?"

"More importantly," said the colonel, "Where are we?"

"We've been stranded out here for months!" Gerald was so excited he was shaking. "We're shipwrecked!"

"Where's the ship?" Sammy asked, as they all tromped over the bridge to the mudroom Mason had designed that formed an entryway where the large hole in the boat had been. Just in front of the indoor lake. Which was now railed off with a wide deck that hung out over the water, and sported a built-in bench and table for Stuart to fish from. There were even racks holding his fishing poles, though he hadn't been there for weeks.

"This is it," said Millie. "We decided to turn it into a lodge, since that's what we came here for. Except we'll probably have to tear it down if we're in a federal wilderness area. Or on someone else's property."

"It's someone else's property," the woman answered, sluffing out of her forest green jacket and hanging it on one of the wooden pegs. They were a striking couple. He was handsome, in a rugged sort of way, and she was quite lovely. Except it was almost impossible to tell how old they were. Not too young, and not too old. It was the oddest thing, Stella thought... maybe because they had such beautiful skin.

"It belongs to some rich-guy who never-comes anymore." Even the woman's voice was lovely. Had a sing-song quality to it.

"So, no worries, eh?" The man gave the colonel a wink and a nudge.

"Well, I don't know about that," he replied. "But I suppose it wouldn't hurt to make an offer. Just for this little piece, anyway."

"You have to find him, first. Right, Mary?"

"Yeah, our family's been living on the other-end, over the mountain. We got a whole village out- there. Both of us were raised-up in it. This is my husband, Sammy Robert. We're middle-age, now, and even we never saw that old-man, yet."

"It's a good place because it's a wild place," Sammy added.

"Oh, I like how you got this all fixed-up!" Mary followed Millie up the companionway stairs, looking everything over along the way.

"Wait till you see the galley," Millie replied. "I mean, the dining room."

Getting ready for Christmas was festive. Or, at least, as festive as it could be with only half a family. It had been nearly six weeks since the *Mah-Bo II* chugged out of the inlet, on a promise to return as soon as possible. There had been several discussions about it. Especially after Gerald, summoning every ounce of courage that remained in him, agreed to ride back to the village—with some others who had dropped by during a hunting trip—and try to make contact with the outside world. The most important thing being to locate the owner of the property they were shipwrecked on and find out if they didn't have enough to either buy, or work out some affordable arrangement to stay.

An idea that became more appealing every day. The remote location, without a single road into it and such a hazardous inlet to get past by water, perched on the very edge of one of the most notorious stretches of ocean in the north country, couldn't be all that expensive. Could it? At least, that's what Stella thought, who had never felt more at home in her life. Or, more safe.

Not to mention they had turned the little spot into something of a paradise they were all growing more and more reluctant to leave. No matter what condition Mason's lodge turned out to be in. Why, it was even better than the *Villa Nofre*. The truth was, none of them wanted to move from *The Last Resort*, anymore. Not when they had settled in so comfortably, could live so cheaply, and —most of all—would still be in the same place, should Cole and Lou Edna ever come back.

They were fairly sure Stuart was no longer with the young couple, or he would have insisted on being taken back to his boat, no matter what Cole and Lou Edna decided do. Which he probably had no idea of, since they would have taken him to a hospital, first. By this time, their former Captain was no doubt wondering where everyone was, and giving care workers a hard time in some rehab center he had been transferred to. Maybe even having to go to a "quiet room" —or worse—if he didn't behave.

Stella worried a lot about that. Because she knew for a fact the most independent patients often lost heart the quickest, when they could see no way out of their situation and simply gave up. Which would be a sad end for the man who had not only made all their dreams possible, but had sacrificed his own most precious thing in the world to do it. Considering the *Dreadnaught* would never go to sea, again, it had truly been his "finest hour."

So, it was on a late afternoon, only two days before Christmas, while Stella and Millie were stringing the last of their Christmas lights around the galley porthole, and waiting for a ham to finish baking, that they heard the drone of another motor in the distance.

"Stuart and the kids!" Millie cried, dropping her end of the lights and grabbing her yellow knit hat and ski jacket from the hooks by the door. "They've come back! Oh, I knew I didn't have Mason make that little wooden train set for nothing!"

Stella climbed down off the counter and reached for her jacket, too (periwinkle blue, with a hood), and had barely joined Millie on the foredeck when she saw that it was just another snow machine, coming through the pass. They had been having quite a few visitors from the village since Sammy and Mary Robert had discovered them. Word had definitely gotten around about Millie's cooking, and it was still hunting season.

"Maybe it's Gerald," she offered. "Wouldn't it be wonderful if he at least heard some news about them?"

"Well, he's—" Her friend reached into her pocket for a tissue and blew her nose. "He's sure had enough time to, he's been gone over a week!"

It was Gerald.

A very excited Gerald who came barreling down through the meadow with some sort of sled in tow, bounced up over a berm, and down again in a puff of powdered snow that caused a delighted feminine laugh to escape the passenger holding onto him from behind. By the time they came to a stop, in front of the bridge, Mason and the colonel had come out to see who it was, too.

"You'll never believe it!" His voice was muffled before he got the helmet off. "Wait till you hear what I found out! This is Sarie, by the way."

By that time his passenger had climbed down and taken her helmet off, as well. "That's short-for Sarah," she informed them. "But he calls-me that." Then she laughed. It was a musical, contagious giggle that set her dark eyes dancing in her round face, and the short black ponytail on top of her head quivering.

"Come and warm up," said the colonel. "I'm sure we've got a kettle on the stove."

"We've got hot apple cider and eggnog, too," Millie boasted. "This being the holidays, and all. But don't keep me in suspense, Gerry—have you heard anything about Lou?"

"In sort of a round about way, Mil," her cousin replied as he undid the bungee cords on the sled and began taking off bundles.

"What is all this stuff?" Mason handed one to the colonel, and then the took another for himself as they followed the group inside.

"Fresh meat for Millie's freezer. Enough to last all winter!"

"Must of cost a fortune."

"Not really. I'll tell you about it when we get inside."

"That's some jacket, too, Gerry. What—was there an ATM machine in that village? It's a good sign Shortcake didn't clean us all out, anyway."

"No, no ATM, I'm afraid. And this is a Native-sewn fur parka," he explained. "Made in one of the villages, up north."

"Must have cost a fortune."

"It was a gift, really. From my..." He set his bundle down once they were inside the mud room and put an arm around Sarie (who was wearing a similar one). "My fiancee!"

"What?" Millie had been halfway to the companionway stairs when she heard it and turned around to hurry back, again. "What?"

"Congratulations! Oh, Oliver, isn't it wonderful?"

Stella felt delighted over the news. Having spent so many years alone and lonely, she wouldn't wish the same fate on anyone.

"We both-like gardens." Sarie giggled, again. "I sell vegetables out of my greenhouse. It's called *Garden by-the Sea*. The whole village buys my vegetables. I brought some for Millie."

"For me?"

"Yeah, it's a present from *Huckleberry Mary's Place*, with a recipe for bear-meat stew."

"Huckleberry Mary? I don't know anybody like that, but it's awful nice of her."

"Oh, you know her, Mil." Gerald helped Sarie out of her parka and hung it up on a peg next to his. "It's Sammy and Mary Robert's new place. She made herself famous using the Huckleberry Betty recipe you gave her."

"She what?"

"From that cookbook you and Stella are working on. The first day they came here. Remember? Let's go upstairs, I'm starved."

"OK, but Gerry don't keep me in suspense. If you know anything at all about Lou and the baby, I want to hear it first thing. I've been half out of my mind worrying about them."

"They're all fine, they're in Ketchikan. Going to try to be home by Christmas."

"Christmas—that's day after tomorrow—Mase did you hear that? By Christmas!"

"That girl's gonna hear it from me, giving us a scare like that," he grumbled as they all filed into the galley. "What have they been doing all this time?"

"Waiting on some tests for Stuart, along with his

physical therapy. He was supposed to be released this week, so they should be here any time."

"How did you find this all out?" the Colonel settled into his place at the table while Stella put the kettle on for hot cider and Millie got out the eggnog. "Talk to them on the phone, somehow?"

"No phone service in-the village," said Sarie. "It's just a little village. Only about twenty-five people."

"That's the thing!" Gerald smacked his hand on the table and laughed. "You better sit down, Mason."

"Now, what did she do." He slid one of the counter stools over and sank down onto it. "Better give it to me straight."

"She did just what she said she would!" Then he turned to his cousin. "What do you think of that, Millie? She hasn't run off or stolen a thing since she left here. She and Cole went looking for the lodge—like we asked them to—and we just missed each other. Well, they were there two weeks, ago. They're back in Ketchikan to shop and pick up old Stuart, now."

"They were at the village?" Mason rubbed a hand over his whiskers. "How did they end up there? Get stuck in weather and have to duck in somewhere close by? That would be a coincidence, all right."

"No, it's even a bigger coincidence. Brace yourself, Mase." Gerald slid behind the table, on the bench next to Sarie. He smoothed down his mustache, laughed a bit (which made Sarie giggle), then finally smacked his hand on the table and shook his head before declaring, "The lodge... is the village."

"What?"

"I could hardly believe it, either! I mean, what are the

odds?"

Millie suddenly stopped shaking nutmeg into a pitcher of eggnog, as if the realization only just registered. "Are you saying Mason owns the whole village?"

"Holy Mackerel—all those twenty-five village people are up there living in my lodge?"

"Well, there's a couple cabins scattered around it, but for the most part, yes."

"They said some old man owned it."

"We're not exactly spring chickens," the colonel reminded him. "But I have to say it is hard to believe we've been sitting on our own land all this time. Harder still to imagine it stretches all the way from the village to here."

"But the village isn't that far away," insisted Gerald. "Just over the hill. Right Sarie?"

"Yeah, and that's the long-way. On the beach, it's just around-the point. Nobody likes to go that way, though. Too many rocks. This side is good hunting, but there has to be lots-of snow. Too much muskeg to get over-that pass the rest of the year."

There was quiet for a moment as all this new information sank in.

Mason realized he still had his hat on, snatched it off, and slid it under his stool. "Guy I got it from told me it was about seventy-eight acres. Last of one of those big homestead plots the state used to give away by lottery. All you had to do was make improvements, and live there for five years, to own it free and clear. So, he built the lodge. After that, he just came back to hunt and fish every year."

"They don't do it that way anymore," said Sarie. "Only sell little pieces around-the towns, now. For lots-of money."

"Way he told it, only a small part of the property was really usable."

"Muskeg and rocks," agreed Sarie.

"That's what he told me. Most up the side of a mountain..."

"Where-the pass is," she added.

"And the other part nothing but rocks and trees. Smack in the middle of a wilderness with no roads. That's what he said. Had to come inland by boat for a few miles, then hike in a few miles more to some lake. That's where the only livable land was."

"Fish Eagle Lake," she said.

"By the hoagie—that's the one. He built his hunter's lodge next to it."

"Old-man Dunny's lodge. He let the families set up fish camp on his-place every year, too. Then when he stopped coming, we just stayed-anyway."

"That was him, all right. Elmer Dunstan. By the Hoagie!"

"I think it's a miracle," said Stella. "Even though we overshot and came in on the back end, we weren't as far away as we thought we were. Just seemed like it in all that fog."

"Things do seem farther in a fog," the colonel agreed. "Especially if you have to inch along the way we did. And we should remember what an excellent navigator Captain Stuart has always been, too."

"Shortcake sure did a good job of tracking the place down for us," said Mason. "It's a real twist about the village, though." He looked over at Sarie. "You people been out there a long time."

"We had to start our own corporation, we're so far

away-from the others. Lots of paperwork. Had to elect a president, too. That's-the rules."

"Certainly sounds permanent," said the colonel. "And if I know Mason..."

"I wouldn't feel right kicking anybody off land they grew up on." The carpenter rubbed another thoughtful hand over his whiskers. "Maybe we can make some kind of deal."

"I already did," said Gerald. "Didn't think you'd mind, old man, considering we'll all be in-laws, once Sarie and I get married. We want to live here at *The Last Resort*, anyway. Right?"

"What kind of deal?"

Gerald laughed (which made Sarie laugh), "That's the beauty of it!" He shook his head and smacked the table, again. "They keep on living the way they like, on their side, and we keep living the way we like over here on ours! If we do that—and this was the president's offer after talking it over with the elders—they'll keep us in supply of all the fish, crab, and meat we'll ever need. What I brought over today, is enough to last all winter."

"Sounds fair enough. Even seems a little heavy on our end, considering the condition of the land. Maybe he just meant for a couple years, then we'd call it even. What with the price of meat these days."

"For as long as they're there and we're here. Talked it over, myself. Right Sarie?"

She smiled and nodded her head.

"I'd feel better if we could meet and shake hands on it." Mason rubbed at his whiskers, again.

At which point, Gerald's new fiancee stood up, leaned over the table, and held out her hand to him.

"Sarie's the president, Mase!" He smacked the table, again. "Nobody else wanted the job."

"Too much paperwork," said Sarie. "We like to share-meat, anyway. Specially, with in-laws."

"Oh, it all seems too good to be true!" Stella set the steaming kettle on a decorative ceramic tile in the center of the table, in case anyone wanted hot cider or tea. "Except for you not getting the restaurant you wanted to start there, Millie."

"I've got enough of a restaurant, right here," she declared. "Look how many customers we've had, already, and the hunting season's still not over, yet. Besides, with Sammy and Mary making my Huckleberry Betty famous, that's all the advertising I need. Almost like having a franchise going in the next town, if you ask me. But how did Lou get anybody to believe her?"

"She looked up the property records over in Ketchikan to find out the exact location, then brought along a copy of the deed. Which, of course, has Mason's name on it. Then when she recognized your Huckleberry Betty recipe at the restaurant, Mil... that's when Sammy Robert told them they found all of us out here. She even left a letter for you before she went back, so you wouldn't worry."

"Lou wrote me a letter? Before Mase?"

"Yes, there's something in it she wanted you to be the first to know." Gerald reached into his pocket and retrieved a piece of paper that was simply folded over. "Of course, it's been read by the whole village, already. Without an envelope and all."

"I read-it twice," Sarie admitted, and giggled, again.

Millie sat down on the end of the bench and started to

read, then burst into tears and handed it off to Mason to read out loud.

> *Dear Millie,*
>
> *It's going to be a girl! I wanted to name her Princess Grace, for an extra advantage in life, but Cole said she had to have an ordinary name, too. So, we're going to call her Princess Grace Mildred DeForio, after the only mother I've ever known. Royal people have longer names, anyway.*
>
> *Cap has a couple more weeks of therapy then we'll all be home for Christmas. Can you believe we've actually been on our own place all this time? How crazy is that? I really think it's a God thing!*
>
> *Love,*
>
> *Lou*
>
> *PS: Don't worry, I've taken care of everybody's business and we still have money left over for Christmas presents. The colonel's going to get a big one!*

Those few lines—as comforting as they were—didn't go a long way toward making any of them feel better about their finances. Typical of Lou Edna, it pleased and horrified at the same time. Especially the colonel, who—rather than anticipating the largest Christmas present, was worried the girl was going to spend all the money he had saved back so he and Stella could make a trip south in the spring, to try and salvage what was left of his writing career.

A thought so troublesome the two decided to stoke up the fire in their own quarters, even though it was late after the long, exciting visit (that included settling Sari into one of the guest rooms) and talk over their options.

"I've come up with a Plan B," he informed her after she had changed into her pajamas and white terry robe with the Chinese collar (she loved getting comfortable before a cozy fire). He smacked his hands together and continued to pace in front of his desk. "Rather than airline tickets and hotels, we can pick up a second-hand RV and drive down. Even if we're at zero, we will have accrued enough by then to afford something. What do you think?"

"I think it's a wonderful idea, dear." She snuggled into her favorite spot on the couch, beneath the rose-colored afghan. "That would save us quite a bit on the accommodations for that conference you wanted to attend, too. The one you've been going to every year."

"That's right, I forgot about that. It would, indeed."

"And I should have a bit more saved up by then, too, don't forget. I'm actually glad I decided not to combine all my accounts before we left, till we changed states, instead. I only gave her one of my debit cards. Thank heavens!"

"Providential. I can see it, now."

"And she really does have a changed heart. Don't you think? So, maybe she'll feel a tap of conscience if she starts to get too extravagant. It is difficult to resist that Christmas shopping frenzy, though."

"God, help us!" It was an exasperated plea. "What on earth could she imagine I would need—at my age—that's big?"

"Maybe it was just a figure of speech," Stella offered. "Like if she buys us all bathrobes, yours would be biggest. Did she get you anything last year?"

"A bottle of *Jim Beam* I'm fairly certain she stole from

some office party."

"Oh, but that was before she changed, so we can't count that."

"Still, the girl has no concept of money. That's something which takes time and experience. The right kind of experience, I mean. She's smart as a whip with numbers, and the inner workings of the banking industry. I can tell you that."

"At her age? Goodness, she's hardly twenty-four."

"She started young."

"Then I suppose we'll just have to wait and see."

9

Christmas at *The Last Resort* was a grand affair. At first it didn't seem as if the DeForio family would make it, considering it began to snow heavily again, on the day of Christmas Eve. However at the sound of an engine (this time, there was no mistaking the familiar thump of their diesel) early Christmas morning, as the *Mah-Bo II* chugged into the inlet, met by a pajama-and-jacket-clad group that formed the welcoming committee on the bridge. Stella got a lump in her throat at the squeal of delight from the Senator as he came riding up the path on Cole's shoulders and suddenly recognized where he was.

He reached out to Millie first, then burst into tears right along with her when she hugged him close (such a sensitive boy!). Then he had to hop from person-to-person and Stella got another lump in her throat just to feel those little arms around her neck, and that silky soft hair against her cheek when her turn came. His tiny black watch-cap (the same as his Uncle Gerald's), fell off in the tumult, and the rest of him was like hugging a pillow, since he was dressed in a blue snowsuit. Lou Edna brought up the rear, hanging onto the Captain, who insisted on walking himself (still aided by that familiar walking stick) rather than being hauled around like so much baggage over the shoulders of his First Mate.

It was a wonderful reunion.

No one went back to bed even though it was barely seven in the morning. Instead, they all retreated to the glass-enclosed stern deck (made from the extra panes scaled down from Gerald's greenhouse that had been moved ashore), decorated with twinkly lights and a tree, along with plenty of comfortable deck chairs for relaxing in. There was even a small wood stove—removed from the Chief Engineer's cabin—to keep the area warm and still be able to enjoy the winter views on three sides. There was a veritable mountain of presents under the tree, too.

The men had brought them in from the *Mah-Bo II*, while the women put on coffee and carried in all the specialties of the holiday breakfast they had prepared beforehand and only needed a quick warm-up. By the time everyone was settled and the Senator (in a new red bunny-suit, without holes in the knees) had happily claimed the unwrapped wooden train set under the tree... the time of reckoning had arrived.

"OK." Lou Edna started. "I know it's traditional for Pop to be Santa and hand out all the presents. But there's a lot of explaining that has to go with these, so I thought I better do the honors this year."

There was a heavy silence as everyone tried to imagine what their own money had bought themselves. Except for Sarie, who couldn't help giggling with a pleasure that transferred over to Gerald, too. Mostly out of nervousness. He never had much money but had confided earlier to Stella that he only hoped there would at least be enough left to buy Sarie a ring. The two of them were sitting together in a porch swing on the starboard end, that had been hung with chains from the ceiling, and had now become the most enjoyable spot out there.

"Mah-Bo," said Stuart (in a tone that clearly meant, get on with it) before taking a bite of biscuit that had smoked sausage and cheese baked into it.

"All right, I am," Lou Edna replied. "Cap wants me to do his first because it's the most important. Which, I'm sure you'll all agree. Let's see..." She turned to the tree. "I gotta find it, first."

At which point the Senator noticed the biscuit and sausage, and—almost without thinking—let go of the end of Mason's deck chair he had been holding onto with one hand, while playing with the train engine in the other, and began to totter across the short space to Stuart. They were his first steps. The women gasped and held their breath, and the two men sat forward, ready to catch, should he fall during the journey. There were no slip-ups. Other than than flinging himself with total confidence onto the single arm held out to him that Stuart caught him up with to bring him safely onto his lap.

"Mah-Bo!" He laughed, and gave over the rest of his biscuit to the little hands. Then ruffled the child's dark curls and whispered, "Mah-Bo."

"Hey..." Cole got to his feet. "Hey, Cap..."

"His first steps!" Millie cried.

"What?" Lou Edna came out from behind the tree with a box in her hand. "I turn my back for two seconds, and I missed it? Do it, again, for Mama, baby—I want to see this!"

But the moment had passed, as he was now more interested in the biscuit. However, the Captain and his First Mate had locked eyes over the top of the boy's head.

"I know what it means," the younger man told him. "I get it."

The Captain smiled a satisfied smile and leaned back in his chair as if greatly relieved. Lou Edna cleared her throat, and for moment, Stella thought the girl was going to get emotional too. But she tucked a few loose strands of blonde hair behind one ear, took a deep breath, and recovered herself.

"I guess that's about as perfect an introduction as there is. Hmm." She cleared her throat, again. "Anyway. This..." She handed the square box to her husband. "Is from Cap to Cole. And I want you all to know that it took me almost an hour last night, for him to explain it to me. I mean, for me to understand what he was trying to explain. Open it up, Cole!"

"For me, huh..." Her husband winked at her from across the room. "I haven't had a Christmas present since I was a kid. Thanks, Cap. I hope it's not a—" He took the lid off the box and saw the Captain's old battered hat lying inside.

"It's a promotion!" Lou Edna exclaimed to his sudden silence. "You're the captain of the *My Boy II!* That's what it means, Cole. Mah-Bo means my boy!"

He didn't take it out of the box right away. Instead, he reached out slowly to shake hands with the old man, then bent down to give him a hug, instead. "I knew what it meant when I saw you pick up the boy, just now. I'll never let you down, sir. I swear."

"You're smarter than me," Lou Edna declared. "He

had to spell it out with the alphabet blocks I was wrapping up for Buddy last night, before I got it right."

The boy flashed a glance back at his mother when she spoke the name he was finally beginning to recognize as his own.

"Ooops!" She covered her mouth for a moment, and then wagged a finger at the child. "But you don't know what those are, yet, do you. Have to wait and see."

So, the pile of unusual gifts began to diminish. Each one well chosen, turned out to be some thoughtful—not too expensive—token of Lou Edna's special appreciation for each family member. There was a new clip for Millie's lovely auburn hair, along with a home permanent kit the girl promised to take the hours to apply for her. For Mason, a set of lined work overalls (for the really cold days), and for Gerald, a packet of heirloom seeds that came from an apple tree next to George and Martha Washington's estate, ordered specially from a seed catalog. For Stella, there was a first edition autobiography of Mary Roberts Rinehart, that much-loved American version of Agatha Christie.

The larger boxes turned out to belong mostly to the Senator (aka Buddy). Big bouncy balls, a riding scoot-along toy that looked like a tugboat, and various other things that would keep him entertained throughout the winter. With each reduction, they all breathed much easier, since no matter what she had bought for the colonel—barring a villa in the south of France—it couldn't possibly bankrupt everybody. Still, Stella could sense that her husband was practically beside himself, worrying over it. Especially since the small box remaining could not possibly hold a bathrobe. There was nothing big about it, at all.

"And now for our wonderful Mr. Colonel!" Lou Edna's eyes were especially bright and mischievous as she picked up the package. "First of all, I have to say how many times you made me nervous when I was sure you knew I was..." She thought for a moment. "Taking advantage of everybody. You won't believe how many times I was worried you were going to tell."

"Well, I thought about it," he admitted, "but there was always something that constrained me."

"I really didn't like you, back then."

"I understand completely."

"But—man—you were the most patient guy in the world. I tried so hard to irritate you, but you never fell for it."

"Oh, you irritated me many times, Lou." He admitted that, too.

Please, Lord, Stella prayed silently, let it be something inexpensive, like a wallet. Or, an item she stole from him and is trying to give back, maybe? The thought of anyone hurting her wonderful husband in any way was almost unbearable (he was such a good man!).

"But you forgave me for all that. I mean really forgave me." She thumped the slender box against her palm as she thought about it for a moment. "And then you trusted me. I don't know why. Pop and Millie—they love me. I don't know why, either, they just do. But you're the first person, in my whole life who ever trusted me. So. I was trying to think of something special for you. Except you seem to have everything, already, and don't really need anything. Then I got this amazing idea. I actually think it was a God thing. Anyway..." She handed him the box. "Merry

Christmas."

"Thank you, my dear," he replied. "I'll treasure those words." He began to take off the wrapping. "And whatever this is, I'm sure it will be the perfect expression of who you are, in every way."

She smiled the sweetest smile of satisfaction (that girl really did have a good heart!) and finally went to sit down next to her little family while the colonel opened the box and looked inside. It was several folded sheets of paper. Stella leaned over his shoulder to see and as he unfolded them, a check fluttered onto his lap.

"What? What's this..." He grabbed Stella's hand and leapt to his feet, pulling her up with him. "It's—good heavens, girl—it's for twenty-five thousand dollars! Where did—"

"Read the papers!" Lou laughed out loud.

Soon everyone else had gotten up, too, and crowded around him.

"*Dear Colonel Henry, Thank you for your decision to become one of our authors of fine literature for boys...* But I only sent them a query, halfway through Canada."

"Keep reading." prompted Lou.

"*It is a privilege to have someone of your distinction to work with, who is willing to take on this special calling to help raise the standards of today's young people.* I don't recall any such—"

"Go on, go on," Now it was Gerald who interrupted. "I say, the suspense is excruciating. A bona fide advance —it's simply splendid!"

"*Enclosed, you will find the advance against royalties we agreed upon...* But I never did!"

"I'll explain later," the girl insisted.

"...with the final installment to be paid on submission of the completed first manuscript, First manuscript? *...previously discussed,* Now, I know I never discussed anything... *and spelled out in your copy of the contract."* He flipped to the next page (it was certainly a contract), then back, again, to hurry through the final words. *"Welcome to you and these wonderful characters you have created. We will look forward to many years of adventures, together.* Many years—good Lord—did you hear that, Stella?"

"I certainly did—many years!"

"Sincerely, E.F. Coffman, Editor in Chief..." He turned to the last page and looked at the signature that he definitely recognized as his own. "I'm thunderstruck! In a wonderful sort of way, but this is entirely impossible. I never in my life signed such a thing!"

"I signed it for you."

"Lou—Edna—DeForio!" Millie gasped and reached into the pocket of her robe for her heart pills. "You. Of all people... should know what forgery is!"

"It's a felony. But Millie, only if someone presses charges, and I knew—under the circumstances— he would want me to! Now, everybody just listen. First thing I did after we got to Ketchikan, was get a P.O. Box and get our mail started up, again. That was on the list, remember? After a couple weeks a big batch of it came through."

"It's against the law to read other people's mail, too," Mason pointed out. "Under any circumstances."

"But there was important stuff in there, Pop. A lot of it had to be dealt with right away, and Cap needed four more weeks of therapy. Four weeks! With no way to get hold of any of you. Besides that, we were getting ready to go looking for the lodge and who knew how long that would take? We didn't even know when we'd get back to Ketchikan, again, much less all the way back here. Millie, if I hadn't ordered you more heart pills, right then? They never would have got there before we left."

"I have been running low on those. I was thinking about that, last week."

"There was lots of stuff like that. But this thing with the colonel—it was time sensitive. I mean, who knows how much paperwork had to go back and forth, or if he took too long to answer and they filled up those slots with somebody else's books?"

"Most definitely could have occurred if I never showed up, again," conceded the colonel.

"See? You did need somebody to handle things for you. That's what agents do. Right? It was sort of like one of those. So, I went ahead and made the deal. A pretty good one, too. If you ask me."

"It's an excellent deal," he agreed. "As long as I don't have to write six books in a year."

"Six books in two."

"It's tight, but I can manage it." He put an arm around Stella and hugged her close. " Now that I have Stel."

"Whew! That's the only part I was a little worried about."

"Well..." Then he laughed at the sheer relief and pleasure of it all. "Lou Edna, I can't thank you enough!"

"Enough to give me fifteen percent? That's what agents get, I looked it up."

"I'll give you ten."

"Woo—hoo!" She looked over her shoulder, where

her husband was standing behind her. "See, Cole? I told you he would!"

He wrapped his arms around her, more as if holding her still than giving her a hug. "All I could see was having to come up with bail money." Then he leaned his forehead against the back of her hair with sigh of relief. "Girl, you gotta—quit this kinda stuff!"

"But, now we can start saving for our fishing license." It was a piece of news that had obviously slipped out, and she quickly scanned the circle of questioning faces around them. "It takes a whole lot of money to fish in this state," she explained.

Cole tightened his hold on her.

"Which we are going to earn every penny of. Ourselves," she assured. At which point she caught Mason's doubtful eye and insisted, "I really mean it, Pop."

"Meanwhile, what happens when the colonel has to sign his real signature on something?" Millie suddenly wanted to know.

"Not a problem, Mil. I've been signing everybody's signatures for years."

Millie automatically reached for the toddler who was pulling at her bathrobe, and lifted him onto her hip before giving an exasperated sigh. "Lou Edna, it'll be a miracle —an out and out miracle—if I even live to seventy, trying to figure you out!"

"You got-the best family I ever saw, Gerry," Sarie observed out loud.

"They're always like this," he replied. "You're going to love it here!"

Exactly the way I have, Stella thought to herself, as she looked around the happy room. It was the first

Christmas she hadn't spent alone in many years. Then it occurred to her how her new life had started during the holiday season, exactly one year ago. Goodness, the Lord had brought her a long way on one simple prayer! She looked up at the colonel, who had risked everything he owned (to rescue her way back then) and wondered if he had any idea...

It had been his finest hour.

***

Winston Churchill (who was quoted at the beginning of this story) had to overcome many obstacles in his life. More than the average person. Born into a wealthy family with a long line of ancestors who had significantly contributed to England's history, he felt—from an early age—the burden to do something significant, too. However, he was often in trouble at school, did not excel in most of his classes, and also had a speech impediment. He was overly emotional, as well, and fought bouts of depression throughout his entire life.

When his father died at the age of forty-five, and seeing that many of the men in his family had a tendency to die young, he assumed the same thing would happen to himself. Which led him to believe that if he was going to make any mark in life, it would have to be while he was young. And the only place to do that was in the military. So, he joined the rifle corps at the age of fourteen, went to military school (he had to try three times before passing the entrance exam), and for the next twenty-nine years, volunteered for every battlefield he heard about.

During this time, he also became a war correspondent for several newspapers and—having been deployed to Cuba, India, the Middle East, Africa, and the Western Front (during World War I)—also wrote books about those campaigns. By the age of twenty-six he had seen action fifty times, been captured as a prisoner of war and escaped, and become popular all over the country both for his bravery, as well as for his accurate descriptions and insights of these battlefields. It was also at this age that he campaigned for—and won—his first seat in Parliament. Throughout the following years, Churchill was involved both in politics and wars, during which he made some significant gains... and many equally significant mistakes. When he finally retired, he was at the lowest ebb of his life.

A period which was later to become known as his "wilderness years."

He retreated to his country home to quietly continue his writing. He had done some good. And he had lived nearly twenty years longer than his father. He was done. Finished. However, when the country slipped into crisis, then the Great Depression—and finally—stood on the very brink of another World War... he was offered the post of Prime Minister. England's highest and most powerful office. Something of an accomplishment in itself, except the country was already in a state that was almost too desperate to survive. So, suddenly—when he least expected it—Winston Churchill was faced with his own "finest hour."

And he was up to it.

Today, he is remembered for his steadfast refusal to consider defeat, surrender, or a compromised peace. Ideals which helped inspire British resistance during the difficult early days of the war when Britain stood alone against Hitler. He is particularly noted for his speeches and radio broadcasts which continued to inspire them until victory over Nazi Germany was secured. Named the Greatest Briton of all time in a 2002 poll, Churchill is still widely regarded as being among the most influential people in British history. One of the best paid writers of his time, he was also awarded the Nobel Prize for Literature, *"for his mastery of historical and biographical description as well as for brilliant oratory in defending exalted human values."*

He lived to the age of ninety.

You can read more about this inspiring man, over at:

http://www.WinstonChurchill.org

A Word About

The Stella Madison Capers...

Dear Readers...

I have known Stella Madison for some years, now. In fact, she has been hanging around the edges of my writing thoughts so long her personality and chatter have become quite real to me. I didn't want to write her story (not then, anyway) because it was such a common one. Where was the adventure? After all, an inspirational adventure novelist needs to stick with writing adventures.

But haven't I always declared that life was an adventure? Of course, I have. I even wrote it on my logo. So, I sent Stella off with a wisp of a story, along with a piece of my mind. Just some little thing for an hour's entertainment, and then went back to working on novels. Oddly enough, I began missing that piece of my mind as soon as she was gone.

There was more to her story, I could tell by the hole that was left when she walked away with it. The truth is, I knew just what would happen if I didn't at least get her settled somewhere. After all, it was me that created her and I felt responsible. Now, there are six Stella Madison Capers (I'm pretty sure that's all of them).

But the thing is this.

Not only has she turned into something of an adventurer herself, she has also managed to tag along on mine. Because I had to continue writing this little "mini-series" as I was on my own true-life adventure, headed north to Alaska with my captain husband, aboard a sailboat called the *Glory B.* Which is probably why Stella ended up taking the same route. Anyway, somewhere along the line our paths crossed and became entangled.

But I will leave it to readers to decide where and when that happened, since I have given up trying to figure it out, myself. I have other stories to write. Meanwhile, thank you so very much for reading this collection of four Stella Madison Capers, which make up *The Voyage of the Dreadnaught...* you are truly the reason I write them!

Lilly Maytree
Aboard the *Glory B.*
Summer, 2014

Our Own Great Alaskan Adventure...

Sailing to Alaska has been a dream the Captain and I had for many years. So many, that when the opportunity finally presented itself it had long since began to fade. But as the idea of fulfilling this long-lost dream renewed its hold, we found ourselves invigorated with new hope and energy in spite of our "advanced years." That is: advanced as far as hauling up sails, manning the helm for endless hours, and traveling through long stretches of wilderness areas—alone—were concerned. We have always loved adventuring.

We named our thirty-two foot ketch *Glory B*. It was a name that most described not only our constant awe at the many wonderful experiences the Lord had blessed us to enjoy, but our philosophy of life, as well. To be honest, when we first began to plan the voyage, I pictured it mostly as one long idyllic vacation that would present the spectacular scenery of the Alaskan wilderness to us in ways few people are privileged to see. All while I was floating along in my own little world and writing stories.

What a shock to discover how huge the world really is... and that it is home to so many hazards. I think maybe if I had known what a grueling struggle against strong currents, choppy seas, and twenty-foot tidal changes it would be, I might have had second thoughts. I did have second thoughts. Except, by that time, it was just as far to go on as it was to go back. And we certainly couldn't spend the rest of our lives on some remote Canadian island. Not to mention, by that time, I was sure many of my friends and business associates thought I was either lost, or dead.

There were also many disasters. Incredible disasters we didn't even see coming. But the Lord had us covered on those each step of the way, considering we actually did make it all those hundreds of miles north to Alaska. In spite of broken propellers, leaky shaft seals, and literally bumping over rocks on a couple of occasions. There were fogs that overcame us faster than we could sneak into some cove to hide in, as well as gale-force storms that kept us at anchor in remote wilderness places for many days as we waited for them to pass. I think I learned more French (a lifelong goal) listening to Canadian weather channels than all my years of checking out foreign language tapes from the library.

Meanwhile, I was busy finishing up my little series of *Stella Madison Capers*: this collection of stories about a rag-tag group of senior citizens who were chasing dreams similar to ours and traveling along the very same route. To say I literally lived in those stories is true in more ways than one. And there came a time when I wondered if I was somehow, subconsciously, influencing our journey by my own overly-active imagination. Because before the trip was over, we certainly experienced *Sea Trials*, came face-to-face with a *Pushover Plot*, got *Lost in the Wilderness* a couple of times, and—at one point—even had to use our *Last Resort*. All the details of which will have to wait to be told in our true-life account of that voyage: *Glory B! 750 Miles of Mishaps and Miracles,* written by the Captain, himself.

However, the recurring thread that runs through all those stories is the vital importance of the scripture which states: *"Call out to me in your day of trouble, and I will rescue you." (Psalms 50:15).* And considering my propensity for trying out the same activities as the characters I write about (to see if they are humanly possible), and the fact that we survived every one of the accidents and disasters we encountered (believe me, I never called out to God so much in my entire life)...

I guess you could say we are living proof of that very truth. The Lord truly does hear us when we call out to Him in our day of trouble, and saves us. He makes no stipulations on that promise, either. There is not even an "except for idiots" clause. And sometimes I think it's those of us who continually get tangled up in stupid things that need Him the most. He even clarifies this fact by saying, *"ALL who call on the name of the Lord shall be saved." (Romans 10:13).* A thought I find extremely comforting in times of stress. Because, while I may not always know exactly where I fit into this great sea of humanity we live in, I at least know I'm human and that the word "all" includes even me.

Thank you, God!

And many thanks to all our dear readers, for following along with us on these adventures.

Lilly Maytree
November, 2014
Thorne Bay, Alaska...still aboard the *Glory B.*

About Lilly Maytree...

Lilly Maytree is the author of *Gold Trap, The Pandora Box,* and *The Stella Madison Capers.* Books that sent her careening along on her "Mystery Tours" with her captain husband aboard the *Glory B.* She loves sharing these adventures with readers. It has even been said that she time-travels (but that's probably just a rumor). To find out about her current adventures, simply visit:

www.LillyMaytree.com.

You can get in touch with her by sending an email to: lilly@LillyMaytree.com. It might take a few days if she is adventuring far away... but she always comes back sooner or later.

Other Books by Lilly Maytree

The Stella Madison Capers...

Home Before Dark
(Caper #1)

Here is the first of the Stella Madison Capers, the story of how everything started, and how she escaped from a catastrophe that seemed to come out of nowhere. Which is the nature of catastrophes but it's so hard to be logical when you're in the middle of one. It's also the story of how she met the colonel (if you're interested in that sort of thing).

A Thief in the House
(Caper #2)

Stella Madison is back, this time with a bevy of friends. But just how far should a person go when it comes to sticking by their friends? There's a thief in the rambling old mansion she moved into. And while it was someone who was quick to lend help when Stella needed it most, how can she possibly return the favor without jeopardizing herself along with them? No person is obligated to go that far... right?

Novels...

Gold Trap

Megan Jennings is headed to Africa for high adventure and divine appointments until she makes a small wrong turn. But what is faith, if not to strike out against impossible odds believing you will win? Or leap out into the dark knowing someone will be there to catch you? Someone does catch her... but it isn't who she was expecting.

The Pandora Box

Journalist D.J. Parker learns the location of a famous cache of diamonds that were stolen during World War II. What she doesn't know is—the federal government has been following the case for years. With an old journal to lead the way, she sets out aboard a yacht that once carried the infamous Herman Goering. A thrilling treasure hunt that could either prove to be the adventure of a lifetime... or her worst nightmare.

For Writers...

Unspoken Rules

Popular books (those stories everyone likes no matter what the subject) all have certain things in common. And what they have most in common is what they DON'T do. Within the following pages, dear writer, you will find the three most important "don'ts" of popular fiction that I learned when I was studying the masters. Why? Because I love research and I never mind sharing my notes.

Writing Rules!
(a mysterious student handbook)

A mysterious little desktop handbook that can help anyone (well, almost anyone) with writing rules. Especially if you are a student and have to write things all the time.

***

Thank you for reading this book! May you be specially blessed knowing that you have blessed others simply by doing so.

9 781944 798062